Comments on L. C. Hayden's
Who's Susan?

Here's one hot damn of a mystery story with a child in jeopardy, amnesia, a chase in the Southwestern desert . . . it's a novel with real people in real trouble. . . . Highly recommended. . . .
New Mystery Magazine

A true thriller, bound to keep the readers' eyes glued to the pages until the final secret is revealed. . . .
The El Paso Herald-Post

Will keep readers turning the pages to its gripping end. . . . ***The El Paso Times***

WHO'S SUSAN? is a suspenseful book that will keep you up until the wee hours of the night just so you can finish it and see what happens. This book is a page turning, non-stop thriller that receives two thumbs up! . . .
The El Paso Observer

WHO'S SUSAN? is compelling, a tightly written suspenseful mystery that keeps you guessing until the end. It's a terrific first novel. . . .
Today's News-Herald, Lake Havasu City, Arizona

Intriguing. . . . ***Sisters in Crime, Austin Chapter***

. . . the suspense has twists and turns that keep you guessing. . . . ***The Monitor, Los Alamos, N.M.***

Who's Susan?

Unable to stop herself, Susan once more mouthed the headline: "WOMAN WITH NO PAST SURROUNDED BY MYSTERY."

She read the article and re-read it, each time hoping that she had misinterpreted it—that it really didn't make her seem to be the number one suspect. But she had talked about blood, and there were the headaches, and Timmy had willingly left with "Mommy." No doubt about it. The newspaper piece, in presenting only the facts, made her look guilty.

The article had of course also introduced the other side. There were many quotes from her colleagues—teachers, administrators, and even some students. They all claimed she was an excellent teacher, a caring person, and above all, "normal." They were all shocked at the accusations.

Susan let the paper drop to the floor as she stared at the wall directly in front of her. I love you, Timmy, she thought. Mommy wouldn't hurt you.

WHO'S SUSAN?

Copyright 1995 and 1998

L.C. Hayden

To Lelly,
It's a pleasure to
know you!
Love,
L.c Hayden
1/'99

Top Publications LTD. Co.

Top Publication's Paperback

Who's Susan?

This edition published by Top Publications, Ltd. Co.

1631 Dorchester Dr., Suite 139

Plano, Texas 75075

ALL RIGHTS RESERVED

Copyright 1995, 1998

L.C. Hayden

ISBN#: 0-9666366-1-9 formerly ISBN: 1-55197-182-8

This is dedicated to my three loves:
Richard, Donald, and Robert.

Acknowledgments

I am indebted to several people for proofreading certain sections of the novel. Their suggestions were greatly appreciated. This group includes Luz Maldonado, Michael Warren, and Dr. Michael H. Moore. An extra hug goes to Ray Whiteman for an overall great job in proofreading.

I'd also like to thank the El Paso Dispatchers and Officer Danny Christman. He took time off his busy schedule to guide me and answer many questions.

A special thanks goes to all of the people at Top Publications, but especially to author and editor Bill Manchee. I appreciate the vote of confidence.

And as always, loving thoughts to my family and friends who provided support and guidance and lots and lots of kudos to Rich, Donald, and Robert. And a very warm and special kudo for my Houston family, Pam Payne who helped out with the original promotion of this book.

Chapter One

Tennis shoes.

Susan Haynes drummed her fingers against the steering wheel as she waited for the light to change. She didn't understand why, but the memory of the tennis shoes bothered the hell out of her. When she had woken from her day-long nap, she found the tennis shoes by her bed.

The light turned green, and she stepped on the gas. She hated the heavy Dallas rush hour traffic—especially today—and thinking about the tennis shoes certainly didn't help matters.

The problem was that she never wore tennis shoes—or any other kind of shoes—inside the house.

Slippers.

She always wore slippers inside the house. Yet when she had gotten up just twenty minutes ago, a pair of tennis shoes were by the bed.

Not slippers, but tennis shoes.

Why? She hadn't been out all day. Early this morning she had tried to get up and get to work, but the pounding inside her head had forced her to spend the day in bed.

Even now she could feel the spidery webs of pain. She shook her head. Lately, her headaches were attacking with more frequency and more ferocity.

She turned the corner and immediately spotted the familiar white stucco building, the Happy Child Daycare Center. As usual, its many tulips and marigolds brightened the place and filled the air with their sweet aroma. When Susan had first seen this place advertised in the Dallas newspaper, the picture reminded her of a fairy-tale building she once saw in a Mother-Goose book.

"Hello, Mrs. Haynes," Dorothy Cortez, the day-care center director, said. She was a plump, tall woman who always found the time to smile. She finished fixing a little girls' pony tail, scooted her back to the playground and turned her attention to Susan. "What can I do for you?"

Susan almost smiled, then realized Miss Cortez was serious. "I came to get Timmy."

Miss Cortez smiled rather awkwardly. "Huh, yeah. Sure." She took a small step toward the back of the daycare center where the four-year old class was held. "I must be going bonkers," she said. "I could have sworn you already picked him up."

Susan shook her head. "No, not yet. You must be thinking about yesterday."

"I guess so," Miss Cortez answered. "I really should take some time off." She winked and left. From where Susan stood, she could hear the TV blaring the theme to *Sesame Street*.

A few minutes later Miss Cortez reappeared. She stood with shoulders sagging, her hands constantly twisting and turning the folds in her blouse. "Can we go into my office?" She tried to sound normal but her voice was too high pitched. "Please," she added as she pointed to the closed door Susan knew led to her office.

A powerful attack of nerves gripped Susan.

"Timmy?" An impatient, nervous edge was evident in her voice. "Has something happened to him?" The room closed in on Susan. "Is he hurt?"

"Mrs. Haynes, I don't know what kind of game you're playing," Miss Cortez's voice was rough and unusually low, "but we don't appreciate it. You know darn well that you yourself came at noon to pick him up."

Susan stood numb, her heart pumping too fast, not quite understanding what Miss Cortez had said. She looked past the director's head. A foot-tall paper cowboy someone had painted was taped to the wall. It had a purple hat. Red hair. Yellow shirt with green sleeves. Purple hands. Red pants. Blue boots. Susan wondered if that was Timmy's. She resisted the urge to run up to the wall, yank it down, and cradle it to her chest.

Her eyes swung back to Miss Cortez. "If I had already picked up my son, then why would I be here?

"I don't know," Miss Cortez answered, then quickly added, "Why don't we go to my office where we'll be more comfortable?" She reached for Susan in order to lead her to the office.

Her touch infuriated Susan. "You find him. And you find him now!" Susan hissed as she repeatedly pointed her finger at Miss Cortez's chest.

"Mrs. Haynes, you were here at noon and you picked him up. Everyone here at the center will swear to that." Her voice was soft, yet emphatic. "Don't you remember coming here?"

Susan remained perfectly still, remembering. Remembering—tennis shoes, not slippers, but tennis shoes.

A tremor glowed deep within her. What was happening? Those damned accursed headaches.

Where is Timmy? Oh, God, where is my son?

Chapter Two

Without asking, Susan picked up the phone in Miss Cortez's office and dialed Jeff's number.

"Dallas State National Bank," the voice over the phone said.

"Betsy, this is Susan. Please get Jeff and hurry. It's an emergency."

While she waited, she could distinctly hear the ticking of the clock, slowly marking the seconds, making them last an eternity.

Finally, she heard, "Susan, what's wrong?"

"Timmy—he's missing."

There was a silence and Susan held her breath.

"What do you mean?" His voice sounded far away.

"I'm here at the daycare center. Timmy's gone. They don't know where he is."

"Hold on, Susan. I'll be there. It's all right. We'll find him. What did the police say?" He spoke rather quickly and in Susan's mind's eye, she could see him, standing up already, reaching for his jacket, putting it on, walking out, even as he talked to her on the phone.

"I haven't called the police yet," Susan said.

"Why not?"

"I want to, Jeff." She looked up at Miss Cortez,

turned, and gave her her back. She whispered into the phone. "I'm afraid. My past."

There was a slight hesitation, then, "Susan, why would you say that? This has nothing to do with your past, does it?"

"No, of course not. I'm calling the police." She hung up and dialed 911.

"My child is missing," she said when asked what her emergency was. She gasped for air and looked up at Miss Cortez who grabbed the telephone away from Susan and gave them the details.

In the meantime, Susan ran out of the office, toward the back where the children were almost through watching Sesame Street. "Have you seen Timmy?" she asked them.

"Yes." That was Brian, Timmy's best friend at the daycare. He was about four inches taller than Timmy, and like Timmy's eyes, his eyes sparkled with mischief.

Susan knelt down so she could be eye-level with him. "Where is he?" she asked.

Brian looked up at the ceiling as though searching for an answer. "You took him home, I guess."

"No, I didn't, Brian." She grabbed his shoulders. "Think. Where is he?"

His eyes grew big and Susan could see panic surfacing in them. "You're hurting me," he said.

"Sorry," Susan said and released him. "I just want to know where Timmy is."

Brian shrugged and ran out. Susan wanted to stop him, but she knew it wouldn't be any use. She looked at the other kids. They stood wide-eyed, staring at her. "Any of you know anything about Timmy?" Some shook their heads, but most looked away. One little girl began to cry.

Susan stood up, walked out, and paced the hallway for what seemed to her to be a lifetime.

"Mrs. Haynes?"

Susan turned. It was an uniformed policeman. Directly behind him stood another policeman. "I am Officer Green and this is Officer Hurd."

Officer Green, a tall, pleasant man with a round face and thick mustache, listened to Susan's story. Occasionally, he jotted down important information. Susan told him how Miss Cortez insisted that she had picked her son up. No, Susan had never had any trouble with her or the daycare center before. Yes, she would swear that she had not picked her son up.

As she spoke, an image flashed before her: tennis shoes. She felt a tautness around her mouth. NO! She had not picked up Timmy.

She had not.

"Mrs. Haynes?"

Startled, she stared at the policeman.

"Are you all right? Would you care for some water? Would you like to sit down?"

"No, I'm fine. I was just thinking...about Timmy."

"Yes, of course. That's perfectly understandable."

"What was it that you asked?"

"I asked if you had a picture of your son."

Susan nodded, reached for her purse, then her wallet. "I always carry a picture of him." She found the wallet and almost dropped it. She took a picture out and handed it to the policeman.

"How recent is it?"

"Very recent. In a week from now, he'll be five years old, and I always have his picture taken prior to his birthday." Susan bit her lip, took a deep breath, and asked, "Do you think he'll...he'll be with us for his birthday?" Icy tentacles of fear touched Susan. She must find him before his birthday. Otherwise...otherwise... Susan shook herself.

The officer put his hand on Susan's shoulder and gently squeezed. "I'm sure we will, Mrs. Haynes." He closed his note pad. "Can we keep this picture?"

Feeling too weary to answer, Susan nodded.

The other officer, Officer Hurd, finished questioning Miss Cortez. The two policemen exchanged a couple of words. At one point they both glanced at Susan. Officer Hurd signaled for her to join him. She followed him to Miss Cortez's office. Miss Cortez sat perfectly still on the edge of the couch, her hands neatly folded in front of her. Her skin was pale, her large gray eyes were glazed as if she was in a trance. She didn't move a muscle, not even to breathe.

My God! Susan thought. She really doesn't know where my Timmy is.

Susan looked around. The smaller kids were playing with some building blocks. The older ones grouped together and whispered among themselves. Two little girls often stared at Susan, sending accusing glares her way.

No one knows where he is. He's gone.

Gone.

"Susan." Jeff stood by the door, his paper-white face reflecting his concern. "Anything?"

Susan shook her head and rushed toward her husband. He greeted her with open arms and Susan collapsed into them.

"Hang on, honey. You've always been a fighter. Don't give up now. I need your strength and so does Timmy." With his arms around her, he led her to the well-worn couch.

Julie, a youthful employee at the center,

handed Jeff a glass of water. "For her," she said, her tone as warm as a glacier.

"Thank you," Jeff answered as he held the glass, forcing Susan to take small sips.

"I'm okay," Susan said. "Don't worry about me."

He set the glass down, took his wife's face in his hands, and kissed the tip of her nose. "We'll find Timmy, just you wait and see. He'll be safely tucked in his bed tonight." He smiled reassuringly, although his eyes told her differently.

Jeff looked up toward the door, noticed the policeman, and patted Susan's thigh. "I'll be back in a second."

She wanted to stop him, to tell him what they suspected. She had to make sure that he believed that she hadn't picked Timmy up. He loves me, Susan thought. He'll believe me. Then she remembered the tennis shoes. She looked down.

"I'm Jeff Haynes, Timmy's father," Jeff said as he approached the officers. "What can I do?"

"I'll be blunt, Mr. Haynes," Officer Hurd said. He stole a quick glance at Susan as though debating whether to continue in her presence. He arched his eyebrows and slightly shrugged. He chose to continue, "Miss Cortez—and also Julie Ward—insist that your wife picked Timmy up at noon. I checked the sign-out sheet and it shows Timmy was picked up at twelve-o'-four."

Jeff's mouth slowly dropped open. He turned to Susan. "Is this true? Did you pick Timmy up?"

Susan shook her head.

Jeff looked up at the policeman. "I don't understand." He mumbled his words, something he never did.

"There isn't much to understand. The sign-out sheet tells us that she picked Timmy up at twelve-o'-four."

"I want to see that sign out sheet," Jeff said.

Officer Hurd nodded and Officer Green handed it to him.

Jeff studied the signature. "It's printed. Anyone can print like this."

The policeman nodded. "I agree, but that is the way she normally signs him out, isn't it?"

Jeff handed him back the paper. "Anyone could have written that."

"True, but that along with he fact that everyone here at the center is willing to testify that Mrs. Haynes—your wife—picked Timmy up only leads to one conclusion."

"I don't understand why they're doing this. My wife would never pull a stunt like this. She adores Timmy." He ran his hand across his forehead. "Isn't it possible they got the days confused?"

"I thought of that and I asked Ms. Ward. She said that it wasn't possible because she specifically remembers that your wife looked rather nervous and kept messaging her forehead as though she had a headache."

Susan recognized the shock in Jeff's face. It was shock born from realizing something one does not—could not—comprehend. "Everyone?" he finally managed to say.

"I talked to the children," Officer Hurd continued. "One of them—" He thumbed through his note pad, apparently looking for some specific information. "Here it is. Jenny. Jenny told me that your wife picked Timmy up today. I asked her how she knew it was today. She said she and Timmy were in the middle of eating their spaghetti when Mrs. Haynes arrived. Jenny said that Timmy started acting funny—'giggly' is all I could gather—when his mom was here, and he seemed anxious to go. But he insisted on finishing his spaghetti because it was Daddy's favorite meal." He closed his spiral notebook. "I checked the menu. They served spaghetti today."

Jeff clenched his fists until the knuckles turned white. "What you are saying..." his voice sounded tight and he cleared his throat, "is that my wife...my wife—" Unable to finish, he threw his arms up in the air and turned, giving the officers his back.

"Did your wife complain of having a headache today?" Officer Green asked.

Jeff turned to stare at Susan. She couldn't hold his stare and looked down as though guilty of something. "Why?" he asked as he turned to face the officer.

"Because Jenny also told me that your wife kept rushing Timmy." He walked away from Jeff's side and stood directly before Susan. "Supposedly, Timmy's mother repeatedly told him to hurry because she had a terrible headache and wanted to get back home."

Outwardly, Susan did not react. But inside, several questions bombarded her all at one time. It was a repeating tape which always finished in the same way. Timmy's mother had a terrible headache. How did Jenny know? Then, the image returned: tennis shoes—not slippers—were by her bedside.

"I think you should go home and wait there. I've called Juvenile Division and Detective Bronson will meet you there," Officer Hurd said.

Susan stood up. She wanted to talk to this detective. Then she wondered what he would say about her past.

A tremor rumbled deep within her.

Chapter Three

Apprehension stretched Jeff's features making him look like a balloon which would explode any minute. "Timmy," he murmured and shook his head.

"What?" Susan asked, coming out of her stupor.

"I was just thinking aloud. Where's our son?"

Susan shook her head and looked out the car window at the changing scenery: strip malls, restaurants, gasoline stations. Oh, Timmy, son, are you all right?

"Susan, we're almost home." Jeff's mechanical tone caused Susan to turn and stare at him.

"I know," she said.

"You do realize that things could get quite ugly—when we get home."

Susan felt her body tense. "What do you mean?"

Jeff let out a long-drawn sigh. "You know what I mean."

"My past." Even to her own ears, Susan's voice sounded timid.

Jeff nodded.

"I swear, Jeff, my past has nothing to do with Timmy." Susan crossed her arms in front of her.

"I believe you, sweetheart, but the fact still remains that the first eighteen years of your life are a complete blank. You don't remember a single thing that happened."

"I know that."

Jeff briefly glanced at his wife. He reached out and gently squeezed her shoulder. "Don't worry, hon, everything will turn out okay."

"I wish I could believe that. Our son is who knows where, and the police are going to look at me as if I did something wrong."

"Maybe not." He shifted uncomfortably in his seat. "I just wonder about those headaches."

"I've been to the doctor—"

"Who said there was no physical reason for them."

Susan shrugged. "Dr. Dwight Orr—"

"Is a psychiatrist. My God, Susan, you're visiting a psychiatrist. How do you think that's going to look?"

"He's trying to help me remember what happened."

Jeff momentarily took his eyes off the road to gape at Susan. "Is that what he wants you to do? To remember? I thought he said that could be dangerous. You could return to your former catatonic state."

"I was eight years old when it happened. I'm a grown woman now. He's sure that under his supervision it's safe for me to remember."

"How successful have you been at remembering?"

"Not very." Susan shook her head. "It seems that every time I try to remember, my head begins to pound so hard that it pushes aside any memory or any kind of thought at all."

"So your headaches are related to your past."

"More than likely, which means that they don't have anything to do with Timmy." Susan looked out the window and sighed. "I just wish I could remember."

"Does that mean you'll be returning to Pine Basin?" Jeff slowed down when he spotted a group of children playing.

"No, I don't think that's likely. New Mexico may be our neighboring state, but it's too far away from here." Her eyes were glued to the group of children. "I need to be here for Timmy."

"Susan, why does everyone at the daycare center claim that you picked Timmy up at noon?" Jeff cleared his throat.

Susan bit her lip so hard, she tasted the coppery bitterness of blood. "I...don't know. I don't even have the slightest clue."

Jeff pulled up into their driveway, turned off the engine, and wrapped his arms around his wife. "For what it's worth," he said, "I know you could never hurt Timmy. I'm just worried about what the police are going to think."

As they got out of their car, a broken-down, early seventies model Ford drove up, and Detective Harry Bronson stepped out.

Susan glanced at him, momentarily closed her eyes, and prepared herself for the worst.

Chapter Four

Detective Bronson was a solidly built man with high cheekbones, coarse black hair and bushy eyebrows. He walked slowly through each room, paying special attention to the pictures above the mantel. "Just the three of you?" He held his hands behind his back.

Susan nodded.

"Nice picture," he said referring to the family portrait in which Jeff was standing slightly above Timmy and Susan. In the picture, as in real life, Jeff's wide, muscular shoulders symbolized his strength. His slightly upturned chin made him look handsome in a rugged way. Both Susan and Timmy were dwarfed beside him.

Susan looked away from the picture. "I like it too," she said fighting the tears she felt ready to form.

"The three of you—you're happy?" Bronson took off his glasses, retrieved a wrinkled handkerchief from his pocket, breathed onto one lens, and cleaned it.

"Of course, we're very happy."

"No reason then why Timmy would want to run away?" He checked his glasses for any more spots.

"None at all."

"Aha." He waited to put his glasses back on before he resumed his walk around the living room. Often his eyes darted from one item to the other then back to the same item. Susan could see he was taking mental notes.

He stood under the archway leading to the hallway. "Mind if I look around?" He didn't wait for Susan to answer. Instead, he headed toward the master bedroom.

Jeff shrugged and followed him. Susan chose to wait in the den. His seemingly endless questions, his studying this or that object aggravated Susan. What did all of these things have to do with Timmy's disappearance?

Susan could hear Detective Bronson in the bedroom, asking questions, storing away more information. A few minutes later, he and Jeff moved to Timmy's bedroom where they spent a lot more time than Susan thought necessary. Finally, she could hear them moving from Timmy's room into the spare bedroom which served as a hobby room. There were more questions. More wasted time. In the meantime, Timmy needed to be rescued. Nothing was being accomplished by searching the house. Susan sighed with frustration. Next came the bathroom. The bathroom! For Pete's sake, Susan thought. What is he expecting to find there? Does he think we are hiding Timmy behind the shower curtain?

Unable to sit passively anymore, Susan headed for the bathroom where she found Detective Bronson going through their hamper.

"What are you doing?" she asked.

"Just looking." He emptied the contents of the hamper and inspected every bit of clothing. Then he refilled it.

"Are you satisfied?" Susan asked.

"Yes," he answered, scratching his chin. "Quite satisfied." As he headed toward the den, he said, "I liked that third room of yours." He arched his eyebrows and cocked his head, pointing toward the third bedroom.

"Timmy loves going in there..." Susan paused. "I grade papers and he, uh..." Susan formed a fist and blew into it, "comes and sits in my lap. He says he's helping me grade papers, but it always takes me more time to grade them."

"You like that?"

Slowly Susan nodded. "The sad part is that I never realized I did."

"We tend to take things like that for granted." He sat down on the recliner.

"I'd give anything if I could tell him how much I enjoyed having him sit in my lap." Susan stared at Timmy's picture.

"I'm sure he knows," Bronson said and leaned back. "I remember when my Carol and me—oh, we must have been married five, six years—we saved all our money to furnish our extra bedroom." He smiled with the memory. "We bought the cheapest bedroom set, but we had the space for the parents to come visit the kids."

"How many kids do you have?"

"Four grandkids—three boys, one girl." He frowned. "I don't get to see them much. One set is in San Diego, the other in San Antonio." He shook his head. "We're gonna go pretty soon, for sure." He sat up straight. "How about you? Grandparents come often to see Timmy?"

Susan shook her head.

"Why not? Do they live too far away?"

"My parents are dead. My mom died when I was seven and my dad died a year later."

"Sorry to hear that. It must have been very hard on you to have your parents die when you were so young."

"I suppose it was."

"So who raised you?"

"I guess you could say I became custody of the state."

"Here in Texas?"

"Later on, yes, but I'm originally from New Mexico."

"Where in New Mexico?"

"Pine Basin, a little town up in the Sacramento Mountains. My parents owned practically every business in town. I understand that if you were to go there, you'll find the McFields Store, the McFields Library, the McFields Park, the McFields Bank." She shrugged.

"If that's the case, how come you're here and not in New Mexico?"

Because that's where my parents sent me, so I couldn't find anything out. Aloud she said, "It's a long, complicated story, and like I said before, it has nothing to do with Timmy. The bottom line is that I don't have any family. It's just Jeff, Timmy, and me."

"No cousins? Aunts? Uncles?"

"None."

"What about you, Jeff?"

Jeff was sitting on the couch next to Susan. He put his hand on his wife's knee and gently squeezed. "Couple of uncles back in Delaware—but I never see them."

"So no chance of a family abduction?"

"None." Jeff's voice was emphatic.

Detective Bronson wrote something down in his pocket-size spiral notebook, then turned his eyes toward Susan. "You wouldn't have any iced tea, would ya?"

"I think so," Susan said. She left and a few minutes later returned with the glass. She handed it to Bronson.

"Tell me, Susan," he stirred his tea, "I can call you that, Susan?" He waited for confirmation.

Susan nodded.

"Good." He sipped his tea. "Good tea." He stared at his glass, as though he was talking to it. "I couldn't help but notice the medicine cabinet. It's jammed full of headache pills: Tylenol Extra-Strength, aspirins, Dristan, Bufferin, sinus headache remedies. Boy, I bet the pharmacy really loves you all."

"What is the point of this?" Jeff asked, a note of annoyance in his voice.

Bronson ignored Jeff and instead directed his question at Susan. "Do you suffer from headaches, Susan?"

For a second she hesitated, then hesitantly nodded.

"Earlier today, did you have a headache?"

"I told you I suffer from headaches periodically."

"Specifically, Susan, today?"

Susan looked down and nodded.

Jeff stood up. "Would you please—"

Bronson waved his hand. "What bothers me, Susan, is that this little girl at the daycare center said you told her you had a terrible headache and wanted to get home."

"You are assuming, Detective Bronson, that I went to the daycare center to pick up my son. At that time, I supposedly mentioned my headache, and Jenny over heard. But since I didn't go, I couldn't have possibly told anyone anything, now could I?"

Bronson raised his index finger to accentuate what he was saying. "But still she did mention the headaches. How do you suppose she knew?"

Jeff threw his arms up in the air. "The hell with the headaches. That's not the issue here. Timmy is. And besides, those kids are friends. Timmy knew his mom hadn't gone to work today because she had another one of her headaches. Hasn't it occurred to you that just possibly Timmy mentioned this to her?"

Bronson nodded. "You're absolutely right. It's possible."

"Look, normally I am a pretty easy-going person," Jeff said. The veins in his neck pulsated, and he held his arms rigid by his side. His hands formed tight fists. "But right now my little boy is missing and I don't see you doing a damn thing—"

"Oh, on the contrary. By now every policeman on duty—and some off duty—have a description of your son. Some even have copies of your son's picture." He smiled. It wasn't the empty type of smile, but the kind a parent would give his child, telling him all is forgiven. "If he's out there, I promise you that I'll personally bring him back."

"What can I..." Susan looked at Jeff, "we do?"

"Stay here by the phone, just in case someone calls. Is there anyone you can trust completely?"

Immediately Kelly's name popped into Susan's mind. Kelly always did what Susan told her to do, and Susan knew she could rely on good ol' Kelly. Why Kelly even wore her hair the same way Susan wore hers—loose and bouncing off her shoulders.

Except—except that Susan wore her hair in a ponytail. Not loose. It was—

A sudden, sharp pain shot through the back of Susan's skull and traveled up and around, centering itself in her forehead. She moaned.

"Kelly. We can call Kelly," Susan said, her hands reaching for her forehead, attempting to massage the pain away.

Jeff's eyebrows knitted as he asked, "Who?"

Susan opened her mouth, but she couldn't remember what she was going to say. She closed it.

"Headache, Susan?" Bronson asked.

She nodded.

"Seen a doctor about them?" He scratched the back of his head. "You know I read headaches can be a sign of real danger."

"Detective Bronson—" There was a note of irritability in Jeff's voice.

"Harry," he said.

"Detective Bronson," Jeff accentuated the word detective, "my son is out there somewhere." He pointed his index finger toward outside. Slowly he brought it down as though feeling defeated.

"Can you call this Kelly person?" Bronson asked.

"We don't know any Kellys," Jeff said.

Bronson thumbed through his pad. "Dumb me. I wrote down Kelly. I was sure your wife said you could call Kelly." He looked at Susan, a question mark stamped on his face.

Kelly, Susan thought. I don't know anybody named Kelly. Susan bit her lip, a habit she had lately acquired when she was feeling tense.

"That's not what you said, Susan?" Bronson's eyes bored into Susan's soul.

"I...I don't know. Maybe. I'm so confused." If only I didn't hurt so much. It was the pain which made me say Kelly. Who the hell is Kelly anyway? "I meant to say Mary," Susan said. "She's my next door neighbor and the closest thing I have to a family. In fact, she's old enough to be my mother, and sometimes I feel she is my mother, although I know she's not." Then to herself Susan added, But she might as well be. After all, she's the one who pulled me out of my catatonic state. I owe her my life.

Susan turned to Jeff. "Do you think it'll be all right to call her?"

Bronson raised a finger as thought asking permission to speak. "Why wouldn't it be all right?"

"Her sister is very ill and she's been out of town taking care of her," Jeff explained. "She really doesn't need another problem—especially since she just finished with a messy divorce. But she would be very hurt if we didn't call her."

Susan noticed that Bronson once again took out his notebook and wrote something down. Susan assumed it was Mary's name. "Logan," she said.

He looked up.

"Her last name is Logan."

"Ah." He wrote it down. "Call this Logan person and see if she can come."

"I'll do that," Jeff said as he headed for the kitchen phone.

"Susan, I want you to write down phone numbers of the people Timmy knows: his friends, classmates, relatives, anybody Timmy might have gone to visit."

"He'd never do that. He knows he's not allowed to go any place without our permission," Susan said.

"True, but he's a kid. Sometimes kids do strange things. Besides, it wouldn't hurt to try, now would it?"

"No, of course not," Susan sat down with the phone book by her side. She jotted down names of people she hardly ever thought of.

The ringing of the doorbell sent a shock running down Susan's spine. She was expecting Mary and knew she would be ringing the doorbell. Yet, when the chimes rang, its very commonness left Susan breathless.

Jeff opened the door and stepped back to allow Mary to enter. Although very athletic, the impression most people got when they first encountered Mary was that she was fragile. Her slim frame, which bordered on being skinny, accounted for this impression, along with her long, oval face. Ten years ago she could have won a beauty contest, had it not been for her hook nose. Even now that her complexion was the color of a clouded glass, she still managed to look radiant. "Susan, Jeff," she said, her voice barely audible. "What's going on?"

"Mary, someone's got my Timmy."

Susan ran to her and Mary wrapped her arms around Susan. They walked toward Jeff and the three of them held each other.

After they disengaged themselves, Mary looked up at Bronson. "I'm Mary Logan."

"I'm sorry," Jeff said for failing to introduce them. "This is Detective Bronson."

For an unusually long time Bronson stared at Mary. "If you don't mind me saying so, you're quite an attractive woman—just like your neighbor here. Are you two related?" He extended his hand.

Mary shook her head. "No, we're not related," she answered as she shook hands with Bronson. "How can I help?"

Bronson handed her the list of phone numbers. "These are Timmy's acquaintances. I want you to call them and see if anybody knows anything." Mary nodded and headed for the phone, but Bronson stopped her. "If you don't mind, Ma'am, please, we'd like to keep this line open just in case someone tries to call," he said.

"Oh, sure, I'll use my phone." She waved and left.

"Is there anything we can do—other than just sit and wait?" Jeff asked.

Bronson nodded. "Make a list of all descriptive and identifying data, including nicknames, birthplace, height, weight, scars, marks, blood type, dental information, anything you can think of, then call NCIC."

"Who?"

"The National Crime Information Center. They have a juvenile branch under their Missing Person File. If they have a match, they'll respond within seconds. If not, it's filed away for future use. All fifty states use them and also Puerto Rico, the Virgin Islands as well as the Royal Canadian Mounted Police." He wrote down a phone number and handed it to Jeff. "Give them a call and if you get anything, give me a buzz."

Jeff nodded as he stuffed the paper into his shirt pocket. "Anything else?" he asked.

"I was thinkin' maybe we could get some copies made of Timmy's picture and put them in all sorts of public places throughout the metroplex. Maybe we'll get lucky and someone out there will see him," Bronson said.

"I'll do that tomorrow," Jeff said.

"Good, let's just hope someone sees him. In the meantime, let's pray for a call." Bronson headed toward the door. As he opened the door, he paused, turned around and added, "You know, this may seem like a stupid question to you, but I don't have any little kids. Mine are all gone and married. Anyway, do little kids nowadays really go around talking about their parents' headaches?"

Without giving them a chance to answer, he walked out.

Chapter Five

Jeff reached into his pocket and retrieved the phone number Detective Bronson had given him. Seconds later he was connected to the NCIC office. He identified himself and gave the woman answering the phone all of the information he had so meticulously gathered.

After she finished recording the information she said, "I'll feed this into the computer and if I get any kind of a match, I'll call you immediately."

"Thank you, and like I said before, tomorrow I'll mail you Timmy's dental records and his picture." He hung up. He stared at the desolate living room and listened to the sounds of emptiness. There must be something he could do beside wait.

His eyes rested on the family picture above the fireplace mantel. He truly loved Susan, and her hidden past had never really bothered him. But now, as he stood staring at the picture, he realized how little he really knew—how little anyone knew. A sudden thought entered his mind and he ran upstairs.

"Susan!" he said as he threw open the bedroom door. She was lying in bed, fully dressed, but not really asleep. "That man who dropped you off—who was he?"

"What man? What are you talking about?" Her eyes popped wide open.

"When you were catatonic someone drove you to Belle View Mental Institute. Who was he?"

"God, Jeff, I don't know. I was eight years old. Why is that important?"

"Suppose he came back for one reason or another?"

Susan shook her head. "No, honey, you're just grabbing at wild straws. My past—"

"I know. Has nothing to do with Timmy's disappearance." He sat on the edge of the bed. "But humor me for a while. At this point we can't afford to disregard any ideas, regardless of how wild they sound." He wrapped his hands around hers. "Sweetheart, I know I promised not to bug you about your past. I know I'm not even supposed to mention it. You said you'd tell me, in your own way at your time. I know all of that—"

"But?"

"I feel you know a lot more than you're telling me. In fact, you haven't really told me anything at all. Don't you trust me?"

She threw her arms around him. "Oh, Jeff, it isn't that at all. Dr. Orr feels it be best if I didn't mention anything."

"Why? What's the big secret?"

"No secret. It's just that he doesn't know much. He went to Pine Basin. Did you know that?"

"And?"

"No one seemed to know anything. I think my parents must have paid them off."

"Everyone? That doesn't make sense."

"Nothing in my past does."

"I wouldn't know about that."

Susan's eyes held Jeff. They narrowed, then opened, then narrowed again. "I'll tell you what I know."

"You don't have to."

"I want to. Maybe it will help me remember." She sat up in bed to tell her story.

Chapter Six

"Dr. Orr?" The man stood in front of the admissions desk. He wore a simple black suit, and Dr. Orr estimated he was probably in his early thirties. "Did Dr. White from Pine Basin notify you that I was coming?"

Dr. Orr stood up and offered him his hand. "It depends. Are you the man who's supposed to bring in an eight-year-old girl, Susan something or other, I believe?"

The man nodded.

"In that case, I've been waiting for you. Won't you sit down?" He pointed to an empty chair.

"No, thank you. I've been sitting down all the way from Pine Basin. If you don't mind, I'd rather stand up." He folded his arms in front of him.

"As you wish," Dr. Orr answered. "Dr. White called two days ago. He said he'd sent the records, but I still haven't received them. Maybe you can fill me in. Tell me about this girl."

"Her name's Susan McFields. A trust fund has been set up under her name. You are to withdraw the monthly fee from this account number." He handed the psychiatrist a folded piece of paper.

Dr. Orr opened it, glanced down at the numbers, and sat back down. "Dr. White explained that.

What I need is information on Susan. What—"

"I understand your need to know, but shouldn't we bring Susan in first? She's sitting in the car, waiting."

Dr. Orr bolted out of his seat. "My God! I didn't know she was out there." He signaled for some nurses to go help.

"While you get Susan, I'll bring her luggage in." The man led the nurses to the car.

Ten minutes later, Susan was in her room, staring at the wall. Dr. Orr stood in the doorway, studying her. There was still so much he didn't know about her. He turned to ask the man some questions about Susan, but he was no where in sight. Dr. Orr glanced up and down the hallway, then headed to the admissions office. He wasn't there either. He checked Susan's room once again. Susan hadn't moved. Dr. Orr went outside. The car was gone. He ran back inside, dialed the Pine Basin operator, and asked to be connected with Dr. White.

"I'm sorry," the operator said, "but Dr. and Mrs. White left town two days ago. It was the darnedest thing. They were here one day, then bang, the next day they checked out: lock, stock, and barrel. Just like that. Gone. Puff. No one even suspected. Do you think maybe they were in some kind of trouble?"

"I have no idea. I never met the doctor."

"Oh." She sounded disappointed. "So what did you wanna talk to him for?"

Dr. Orr hesitated for a fraction of a second, wondering how much he should tell her. "Actually, I wanted some information from him. Maybe you can tell me whom I can talk to."

"Ooooh." It was obvious she enjoyed gossip. "What kind of information do you need?"

"It concerns an eight-year-old girl. Her father just dropped her and he—"

"Are you talking about Susan?"

"You know her?" He felt relieved.

"Who doesn't? Her parents owned practically the entire town."

"Could you tell me how I can get in touch with her father or mother?"

"That's going to be impossible to do."

"Why?"

"Mama died less than a year ago, and the dad— he shot himself. Right in front of Susan too. Poor child. She just turned into a vegetable, I hear tell."

"Then the man who brought her over was not her father."

"I guess not."

"Do you have any idea who he might be?"

"How could I? I don't even know who you are."

Dr. Orr smiled. "My name is Dr. Dwight Orr. I'm calling from Dallas. Someone just dropped Susan here at the hospital. He was a distinguished looking man. Brown hair. Brown eyes. Early thirties. Almost six feet, slim. I need to know who he is."

"Sorry, can't help you. Don't know anybody like that, and I know everybody in this town. And if I don't know him, nobody will. I know everybody— especially all of us who hung around the McFields."

"That's Susan's family."

"Yep."

"Then you could tell me who would be the best person to talk to about Susan."

She was silent for a minute. Then, "No one that I know of. Her parents are dead. She got no other family. Believe me, save your time. No one is going to talk to you."

"Why? What's the big secret?"

"No one knows. The only person who knew was Susan's father and when he killed himself, he took all he knew to the grave."

"His death was a suicide then?"

There was a small pause. "It was an accident. And that's all I know."

The line went dead.

Chapter Seven

"Dr. Orr seems to think that what I can't remember is directly tied to the reason why my father ended up killing himself." Sometime during her narrative, Susan had gotten out of bed.

She stood in front of the mirror, staring at herself, "What did I do, Jeff, that caused my father to kill himself?"

Jeff reached out for his wife and held her in his arms. "Susan, don't say that. You don't know that you caused you father's suicide."

"Oh, yes, I do, Jeff. At first I had my doubts, but now I know. I caused my father's death. And now Timmy...Timmy." She pulled away from her husband and gave him her back.

"What are you saying, Susan?" He walked around her and faced her.

"I don't know. I don't know. I don't know what I'm saying. I don't know what to think. I just wish Saul had dropped me off in the road somewhere instead of taking me to Belle View Mental Institute."

"Who dropped you off?"

"Saul, our chauffeur."

"I thought you said you didn't know who he was."

Susan's eyes widened, and her mouth slowly dropped open. "It just came to me now. I swear to you, I didn't know. God, what else can I remember?"

"Why, all of a sudden, is it so important for you to remember?"

"Because Timmy's gone. Don't you see that?"

"No, I don't see that. You swore to me several times this had nothing to do with your past."

Susan looked down and hung her head.

Jeff quietly walked away. Once downstairs, he headed for the kitchen. It had been a long time since he'd had a drink, but tonight he searched the refrigerator for the one bottle of beer he knew he had left over from their last party. He found it behind last night's leftovers.He opened it, turned on the TV, and flopped down in this favorite recliner. He stared at the TV, but his mind only registered images. Susan knew a lot more about her past than he had realized. Why hadn't she told him any of this before? What else did she know? What was she hiding?

Jeff took a large gulp of his beer and switched channels. Another thought erupted in his mind. He tried to force it away and, instead, concentrate on the program. But the thought persisted, and like a scratched record, it continued to repeat itself: Susan herself picked Timmy up today at noon.

Picked Timmy up.

Timmy...

Disgustedly, he drank the last of his beer. "Oh, Susan," he said loud enough for only him to hear, "what have you done?" He hurled the empty beer bottle. It bounced off the living room wall and clattered to the floor.

Chapter Eight

The sound of shattering glass jarred Susan from a nightmare-plagued sleep. It was not the type filled with monsters and other hideous creatures, but the kind that left her cold and breathless. Death had come and caressed her body. It had whispered something in her ear. A warning, perhaps.

Susan shook off the feeling as she slowly opened her eyes.

She had seen Death.

Susan sat bolt upright. Timmy!

Were her instincts telling her he was dead? A chill shrouded her body and she wrapped her arms tightly around herself. Yes, she had seen death. But not Timmy's.

It was...

A small pounding at her temples forewarned her of the coming of yet another headache. Susan decided to ignore it and instead concentrate on the image.

The image of...a small girl.

The pounding inside Susan's head increased.

Pretty girl.

Kelly...Kelly...Maynard. She had been Susan's childhood friend. They were only eight then. In spite of her worsening headache, Susan began to remember...

* * * *

It had been a Saturday morning, a beautiful, unusually warm, spring day. The sun's rays filtered through the pines, casting odd-shaped shadows on the canopy bed Susan's mom had so meticulously chosen just for her.

Susan was anxious for Kelly to arrive so she could tell her the fabulous secret she learned. She wished, not for the first time, that their estate wasn't so large. Then she could walk to Kelly's instead of relying on Saul, their chauffeur.

Susan heard a car door slam and looked out the window. Kelly and her mother were walking up the driveway. Susan ran down the stairs to greet them.

"Mrs. Maynard, how lovely you look today," Susan said.

"Now, isn't that sweet?" She smiled kindly at Susan then looked disapprovingly into the corner.

* * * *

Susan remembered following her glance...

It was dark and dusky, and now, almost twenty years later, Susan couldn't remember what she was looking at. All that Susan could easily recall was Mrs. Maynard's green eyes staring at the shadowed corner with all the warmth of a frozen food locker.

Susan jumped out of bed and paced the room. She tried to concentrate on that corner.

She closed her eyes tightly. "Look in there, you can see it," Susan told herself. She saw the shadow move.

Susan closed her eyes tighter.
Concentrate.

There was...

The heavy throbbing in her brain weakened her will to continue, yet Susan tried to ignore it and instead turned her attention to the shadow... No, no, it wasn't a shadow. It was a...a what? It was so dark in that corner.

The pain blurred Susan's vision and she sucked in her breath as she massaged her temples.

Again she attempted to focus her eyes. She could see that the shadow was rather large. Three feet high? Bigger?

Susan's head pounded so violently that she cradled it in her hands. Automatically she wobbled toward the bathroom and gulped down two Tylenol Extra Strength tablets. Hoping the dizziness and pain would subside, she walked slowly out of the bathroom, her hands clenching her head.

She almost reached the bedroom when the ringing of the phone sent an electric shock throughout her body. For the moment, her headache was forgotten—or at least pushed aside—while she ran to answer it. She grabbed the handle desperately, willing the phone to continue ringing, afraid that whoever was calling would give up.

Both Jeff and Susan answered at the same time. "Hello?" they said in unison.

"Jeff, Susan," came the voice over the phone. "It's just me, Mary. I just wanted to know if there was anything else I could do."

Susan heard Jeff hang up the living room extension. "No, I don't think so," she said.

"Are you going to work tomorrow?"

Susan hadn't even thought about her teaching responsibilities. "I better stay by the phone," she said, "just in case."

"I'll call in for you," Mary said.

"I'd appreciate that," Susan answered. "Tell them that my lesson plans are all done for about a month. The sub should have no trouble following them."

"I'll tell them, Susan, and truthfully, I'm worried about you. Would you like for me to spend the day with you?"

"I think Jeff will stay. There's no use you missing work on my account. But I'll call you if I need you. I appreciate the offer."

"I'll be waiting for your call," Mary said. "Try to get a good night's rest."

"I will," Susan promised even though she knew that was a lie. She hung up the phone.

In spite of her pounding head, she tried to think about Kelly, her soft, brown hair cascading past her shoulders. Kelly had often cursed it because it wasn't blond like Susan's. "But other than the color, your hair looks just like mine," Susan had assured her, and Kelly had smiled.

* * * *

Susan stood in front of the dresser staring at her reflection in the mirror. She still kept her hair shoulder length, but now it was brown with just a small touch of golden highlights. She knew a lot of people whose hair color had changed as they grew older. She wondered when hers had changed.

Susan massaged her temples and returned to bed. Why, after all these years, had she remembered Kelly? Why now? It's almost as if my past is coming back to haunt me, Susan thought. Is there a connection between Kelly, my past, and Timmy's disappearance? The possibility left a chill in Susan's body as though she had been touched by the fingers of Death.

Chapter Nine

Susan was still resting when the ringing of the doorbell caused her to bolt out of bed. She stared at Jeff, but he was still asleep. She envied him even though she knew he had tossed and turned all night.

As she ran to the front door, she put on her robe, then swung the door open. "Mary!" She signaled for her to come in.

"I had to come," she said, apologetically. "Have you heard anything?"

Susan shook her head and led her to the kitchen. "Join me for a cup of coffee." As Susan poured some water into the coffee maker, she said, "I'm really glad you came."

"I just wish there was something I could do, because I feel so...so helpless."

"Just your being here helps. You've always been here for me." Susan plugged in the coffee maker, and although she was looking at Mary, she was seeing past her. "Sometimes I wonder if that's the way it was between my mother and me."

Mary's shoulders dropped as her face froze in an expression of infinite sadness. Then she shook herself.

As Susan was reaching for the cups, suddenly

she stopped. "Mary, you knew her. Didn't you?"

Like a child caught with her hand in the cookie jar, a startled, frightening look crossed Mary's face. "Huh, no. No. Of course not. How could I possibly have known her?" She wet her lips and looked away.

"I don't know." Susan felt a tremor ignite deep within her. "I get these feelings every once in a while. Please, Mary, if you know about my parents, tell me."

"You got enough problems now without adding your past. Some things are better left alone. Remember, that's what Dr. Orr told you."

"Back then, yes. Now he says it's time for me to remember."

"No, Susan! Don't do that!" Mary attempted to soften the harshness in her voice with a smile, but all that she accomplished was a nervous tremor of the lips. "What I mean is that you need to devote your energy to finding Timmy instead."

"What if the two incidents are connected?"

"That's the most ridiculous idea I've ever heard!" Mary grabbed her purse and abruptly said, "I better go. I'll be late for work."

Susan glanced at the coffee maker and noticed that it was almost ready. The aroma of freshly perked coffee filled the roomy kitchen. "But the coffee," Susan protested.

Awkwardly, Mary hugged Susan. "Save me a cup. I'll drink it tonight." She turned to leave, but at the last moment hesitated. "Please, if you hear anything—"

"I'll call."

Long after she had left, Susan stood by the window, staring out. Her thoughts were as jumbled as an undone crossword puzzle.

* * * *

No sooner had Mary left than Bronson arrived. "I'm trying to tie loose ends," Detective Bronson said as a way of explanation. "I need to check on family members."

The mere thought of discussing her family members made Susan feel as if she had swallowed an active volcano. "You asked us about family members yesterday, and we told you there were none."

Bronson put his opened hand on his cheek, pouted and nodded. "You know, I think you're right." He sniffed around him, like a hound on a scent. "Is that coffee I smell?"

Susan nodded.

"Good. Why don't you get us two cups and we can drink it while we talk about the family. I got this blue form that I gotta fill out in triplicate, and I need just a little bit more information. Now, about that coffee."

"I'll get us some," Susan said, expecting him to wait in the living room while she prepared the coffee. Instead, he followed her right into the kitchen.

As he sat down, making himself at home, he said, "So tell me about Jeff's family."

"His father deserted them when Jeff was only two. Jeff hasn't heard from him since then." Susan took down two saucers.

"Jeff."

Susan looked at Bronson, rather puzzled. "Yes, my husband, Jeff."

Bronson shook his head. "No, I mean, Jeff's father's name is also Jeff."

Susan nodded. "How did you know?"

"Simple deduction." He took out his note pad

and wrote something down. "How about Mother Jeff?"

"She never remarried and last year she died from cancer. Timmy misses his grandma a lot." Susan filled the coffee cups and handed one to Bronson. "There are no brothers or sisters, but there are a couple of aunts, uncles, and cousins—all, or most live in Delaware. We never hear from them, except for an occasional Christmas card."

Bronson took a sip of coffee. "This is good coffee," he said. "I'm gonna have Carol call you up. She's a good woman, but she makes lousy coffee." He took another sip. "It needs cream, though."

Susan stood up to get the cream container out of the refrigerator.

"And your mom and dad?"

Susan froze on her way to the refrigerator. My mom. My dad—Daddy. He was a big, gentle man with a wide, comforting smile. I would often run up to him so he could hug me, and I'd feel safe.

There weren't that many times I felt this secure, even though I knew Daddy was always there to comfort me. Other people apparently felt the same way because Daddy, besides being the sheriff, was the real town leader, and everyone loved him, and he loved everyone back.

Well, almost. Although he did his best not to show it, he didn't love—no, that's not right. He feared because he knew there was something deathly wrong with—

Immediately a pain shot up Susan's neck filling her head with such a loud throbbing noise that it momentarily left her dizzy. With shaking hands, she reached up to massage her temples.

"Susan, are you all right?"

Bronson's voice brought her back to the present. Confused, Susan nodded. "I was just reaching for the cream when the pain hit me."

"Is there anything I can get for you?"

"No, I'm fine." She opened the refrigerator and searched for the cream.

"You were going to tell me about your parents," Bronson said.

Susan held her breath and said, "As I told you before, they're dead."

"You know this, for a fact?" His face betrayed no knowledge, no feelings.

His chiseled looks gave birth to Susan's jittery nerves. She felt that she was slowly losing her confidence. It was like trying to hold on to a fish in the middle of a stream. "Why, yes, of course." Her voice came out too rough.

"You learned this while you were at Belle View Mental Institute."

Susan dropped the ceramic creamer. Its shattered contents splattered all over the cabinets and dining table. "Damn," she said and bent down to clean it up.

Detective Bronson reached for some napkins and began to help her wipe the mess. "Why didn't you tell me you were under psychiatric care?"

Susan bit her lip, trying to keep any type of emotion from escaping. "I didn't think that was important." She kept her eyes glued to the floor.

"Aha," Bronson said.

Susan could feel his eyes fixed on her, constantly analyzing, categorizing, filing information away for future use. Susan continued to move the dish cloth around in wide circles, attempting to clean a floor she knew was already clean.

"So tell me about Belle View Mental Institute," Detective Bronson said as he dumped the wet napkins in the trash.

"Why?"

Both Susan and Bronson looked up to see Jeff standing in the kitchen doorway, his large frame almost filling the opening. His forehead was knotted, his hair ruffled. His complexion, always glowing with a healthy tan, now had a bluish cast as if he were sick. Dark blue smudges like bruises formed half-moons under his eyes.

Bronson dried his hands by rubbing them on his pants. "You look like hell," he said.

"Tell me something I don't know," Jeff answered. "I feel like hell." He walked over to where Susan was and gave her a kiss. "You don't look much better than I feel."

"Thank you," she said.

Jeff smiled an empty smile. He turned his attention to Bronson. "Tell me—us—how my wife's background affects your search for Timmy." He choked on his son's name.

"It doesn't look good," Bronson said. "We have absolutely no indication that the daycare did anything wrong. On top of that, we have several witnesses who are willing to testify that Susan picked Timmy up." He stood up and rested his palms on the counter, as though he needed support. "On the other hand, Susan's been institutionalized and—"

"Susan was institutionalized because she suffered a traumatic experience as a child." Jeff's tone was more authoritative than apologetic.

"And what was that?" Bronson directed the question to Susan who deliberately made a big production of standing up and putting the dish cloth inside the sink.

"I don't know," she finally said. "I—I wish I did."

Bronson stared at her for an unusually long time. Slowly he said, "Tell me about Kelly."

"Who?" Jeff asked, but Bronson ignored him.

He continued to hold Susan's eye.

"She was one of my childhood friends."

"How long have you known about her? Since you came out of your catatonic state?"

"No, I only remembered her yesterday."

"Why yesterday?"

Why? Because...because I was looking for comfort and she always...always...

I was going to say always gave me comfort. But no, that's not really true. I have two opposing pictures: a sweet, lovable, dependable Kelly, and the girl with deep blue eyes, eyes made of crystal. A girl who laughed at me and betrayed me. How can one person be at such opposite ends of the spectrum of friendship?

Susan shrugged. "I don't know why I remembered her yesterday. I suppose each day I'm beginning to remember more and more."

"Do you think that your past and Timmy's disappearance are related?"

"Oh, no! They are two totally different things. What possible connection could there be?"

"You tell me, Susan, because right now I've got this gut feeling that you know a lot more than you're saying—or at least a lot more than you think you know."

Susan looked at Jeff. He was staring at her curiously, then, as though realizing Susan needed his strength, he walked over to her and put his arm around her. "You're crazy," he told Bronson. "You're just trying to grab at straws."

Bronson nodded. "Maybe. Maybe I am. But don't say I didn't try to warn you."

"Meaning?"

"Meaning that it won't be long before the newspapers pick up the story and the public starts reading between the lines." He pushed his coffee cup away and stood up. "They'll crucify Susan, claiming that she harmed Timmy. Pretty soon the district attorney will be pressuring me to arrest her." He turned to leave but not before he added, "If you ask me, it doesn't look good at all."

As soon as Bronson left, Jeff pulled away from Susan. Without saying a word, he started to walk out of the kitchen.

"Jeff," Susan called.

He stopped but didn't turn around.

"Jeff, you believe me, don't you?"

He shrugged and continued to walk away from her, his shoulders slumped.

Chapter Ten

Dr. Orr, a small, balding man, studied Susan through his wire-rimmed glasses. His fingers formed a teepee and he placed them under this chin. "Go on," he said.

"I feel it's time for me to face my past and I need your help." Susan wanted to convince him—to show him—how important it was, but she couldn't even look him in the eye. Instead, she glanced around his familiar office.

His oversized desk, filled with papers, somehow didn't look as threatening as when she was a little girl. Her eyes drifted toward the row of file cabinets. Idly, she wondered how thick her file was.

"You think you're ready."

"Very much so."

"I don't." Dr. Orr stood up and walked around his desk. He half sat on his desk, facing Susan.

"I beg your pardon?" Susan played with the pleat of her blouse.

"Susan, listen to me carefully. When you were a little girl, something awful happened to you. Something so awful that your mind completely shut down. It took you almost ten years to return to normal. Give it time, Susan. You're just not ready. When you are, it'll all come to you naturally."

"But—"

Dr. Orr waved his hand. "I'm not finished. If it's not done gradually under the best of conditions, you could easily return to that never-never land and this time, you might not come back."

"Then make them the best of conditions. You could hypnotize me and regress me a little bit at a time."

"I could, but I won't. These are not the best of conditions. Your son is missing and your mind is with him, not your past."

"But it is with my past." She had to make him understand.

"Explain."

"You know that I have always had a kind of sixth sense. And right now my intuition is telling me that the only way to get my Timmy back is by confronting my past. That's why I'm here, begging you for help."

Dr. Orr frowned. "Susan, you're laying it on thick. But as your doctor—and as your friend—I can't let you risk it. Right now you want your son back so desperately that you're willing to do anything. But this is not the right thing to do. I'm sorry, Susan. After Timmy is returned to you—when you're free from all stress—we can start. But right now, no."

Susan swallowed hard and nodded. "I understand." She stood up. "I suppose that even before I came here, I knew what your answer was going to be."

Susan let herself out and with fast, determined steps headed to her car. With or without Dr. Orr's help, she would find her past.

Chapter Eleven

Four hours had come and gone and the phone hadn't even rung once. Yet, Jeff had promised Bronson that someone would always be available to answer the phone. "Then ring!" he screamed at the phone.

The phone did not ring, but the doorbell did. It was Bronson. He looked on the tired side and not the least bit animated. "No news," he said as he walked in. "Nothing." He looked around. "And Susan?"

"She...uh...had an errand to run."

Bronson's eyebrows furrowed. "Oh?"

"All right," Jeff said, not wanting to mislead him. "She went to see Dr. Orr."

"Her psychiatrist."

Jeff frowned inwardly. "Yes."

"And you're stuck baby-sitting the phone."

Jeff smirked. "It's ironic, isn't it?"

"What's that?" Bronson sat down.

"Two weeks ago Timmy woke up with a stomach virus and a slight fever. My wife was reviewing with her classes and she felt that a sub couldn't possibly do an adequate job. So she asked me to stay with Timmy, but I refused. I'm up for a promotion and missing a day wouldn't look good." Jeff nodded as the guilt ate at him. "So we sent him to the daycare center, and now that he isn't home, we are both staying here."

"I see that a lot. We take so many things for granted." Bronson took out his spiral notebook and scribbled something down. He read what he wrote then said, "Tonight I'm going to tell my Carol how much I love her." He put away the notebook.

The door opened and Susan walked in.

"Susan," Bronson said, "I've been waiting for you."

She stared at him blindly, her mouth slightly ajar.

"No news on Timmy," he said. After a short pause, he added, "Do you have some tea?"

Susan set her purse down and nodded.

"Is your tea as good as your coffee?" Bronson asked as he followed Susan into the kitchen. Jeff threw his arms up in the air, stood up, and made it a three-person procession.

"I suppose," Susan said. "It's sun tea."

"Sun tea," Bronson said as though it was a new revelation. "I'll have to tell Carol that."

After the tea had been served and everyone sat around the small dinette table, Bronson said, "It's been twenty-four hours since Timmy's disappearance." Bronson sipped his tea. "One of the TV reporters got a sniff of the story. But as a special favor she's holding on to it, provided she gets an exclusive. I was hoping someone would call, but if they haven't by now, chances are they won't. I would advise you to go public."

"I see no problem with that," Jeff said. "I'll call that reporter right now." He stood up.

"It's not that simple." Bronson handed Susan his glass for a refill. "Both of you, together, need to weigh your decision very carefully."

Jeff sat down. "What does that mean?"

"There's always the possibility that the press will find out about Susan's past." He paused, taking his time to sip his tea, allowing them ample time to digest his statement. He placed his glass on the table. "When that happens, they'll play it up for all it's worth."

Jeff and Susan exchanged looks. Jeff read Susan's thoughts just as clearly as if she was shouting them out. "I'll make that call now," Jeff said.

Chapter Twelve

Because Bronson had advised them to always have someone by the phone, the interview was to be held at the Haynes' household. At 3:29, the door-bell rang. Jeff opened the door and the lady before him introduced herself.

"Hi, I'm Patricia Berg, CBS news." She was a tall, skinny woman with a hook nose. She pointed to the man standing beside her. "This is Marc Gutierrez, my cameraman." He was several inches shorter than Patricia, but he was a stocky man. "I'm sorry—we're sorry—to hear about your son."

Jeff nodded and let them in. "I just hope this helps bring him back." He hugged Susan.

"Me too," Patricia said, looking around the room. "If you don't mind, I'd like to have you both over here by the couch." She walked over to the bookcase and pointed to a picture of a smiling boy. "Is this Timmy?"

Jeff nodded.

"Cute kid," she said. She picked up the picture and set it on the stereo unit by the couch. "Mind if we put it over here? This way he'll be in the background while we interview you."

"That's fine," Jeff said. He noticed that Marc was holding a power cord in his hand looking for an electrical outlet. Jeff showed him where one was. Marc plugged in, moved some furniture which was in his way and proceeded to set up the lighting fixtures. Fifteen minutes later, they were ready.

"Let's get started."

Pat stood up and Marc focused the camera on her. She straightened her hair, cleared her throat, and stared into the camera. When Marc gave her the signal, she started, "Normally this house is filled with the type of laughter and noise that only a child can bring." The camera panned around the living room. "But today, it is quiet, for yesterday, four-year-old Timmy Haynes disappeared from his daycare center." Marc turned the camera so that the eight-by-ten picture of Timmy filled the screen. "The police have not ruled out foul play, and an intensive search is being made here in Dallas as well as its surrounding cities." As Pat sat beside Jeff and Susan, she said, "I'm sure our viewers' hearts reach out to you, and they'd like to know if there's anything they can do to help."

"Yes," Jeff quickly answered. "They can take a close look at every little boy who's about four feet tall and see if he's our Timmy." He turned to look at Susan, and Pat turned her attention to her.

"Tomorrow we're going to start putting up posters of Timmy every place so that everybody can recognize his face." Susan shifted positions, feeling uncomfortable in front of the camera. "I suppose that if anybody wants to help, we can use volunteers to help us with the posters. We plan to put them up every place here in Dallas, as well as Fort Worth and all the vicinities. That means that we'll need a lot of volunteers."

"Where can people go to get these posters?"

Jeff and Susan exchanged looks. "They can come here to our house," Jeff said, "tomorrow at ten-fifteen. Our address is 6892 Wayland Street."

Pat nodded. "Do either of you have anything else you would like to say?"

"I do." It was Susan who spoke this time. "If you've got our Timmy, please, please, don't hurt him and return him to us. Timmy, if you can hear us, we love you. We miss you. Please come home."

Pat stood up and gave her closing remarks. Neither Jeff nor Susan heard much. They were busy, holding each other, comforting one another.

＊ ＊ ＊ ＊

That night Jeff stayed up to watch the television coverage of Timmy's kidnapping. Susan chose to go to bed early. She wanted to think about her past.

Unfortunately, Susan felt she was making no progress. Maybe she was trying too hard—or maybe not hard enough. It was like trying to work a puzzle with three-quarters of the pieces missing.Determined to find the answer, Susan grabbed hold of one of those puzzle pieces, the one named Kelly. If only she could talk to her, some more of the mystery would be unraveled.

Susan stared at the phone and with shaking hands dialed the Pine Basin operator. "I need Kelly Maynard's phone number please."

There was a short pause while the operator checked for the number. "I'm sorry, but I don't have any listing for any Maynards," she said.

Hope drained from Susan like a sponge being wrung out. "Are you sure?" she asked.

"I double checked and I still couldn't find any." There was an edge of irritability detectable in her voice.

"Do you know anybody who might have known

a Maynard who lived in Pine Basin? They would have been there a little over ten years ago," Susan said.

"Honey, I've been here for over sixty years. If I don't remember any Maynards, nobody will."

Susan thanked the operator and hung up. She had met with a small defeat, but in spite of this, she recognized that the victory had been greater. She had actually contacted Pine Basin. Soon, she promised herself, she'd return to her childhood hometown. In the meantime, she'd stay home in case Timmy...Timmy...

She had to discover the truth behind her past if she expected to get Timmy back. She closed her eyes, trying to form an image in her mind.

She saw...a trail. Or at least what seemed to be a trail. The ancient path led from her house deep into the woods. In several places the brush had grown over the path, concealing portions of it and eradicating the rest.

Except that Susan knew it was there. It had been used by the miners who were searching for their fortunes deep in the forests of what is now Lincoln National Forest.

She was the only one who could follow this ancient trail. It was as though the ghosts of all of those miners were drawing her deep into the forest. She could hear their voices calling her, guiding her.

Chapter Thirteen

Mary turned off the television and silently said a prayer for her neighbors and another one for Timmy. Tomorrow she would devote her time to helping Jeff and Susan in any way she could. She sighed and headed to the bedroom.

The jingling of the phone made her immediately think of Timmy. She quickly picked it up.

"Mary? It's me, Carla."

Automatically, Mary felt her body tense up. She knew this telephone call would come one day, but she hadn't expected it. Not today. "Are you calling from Pine Basin?"

"Yes."

Mary frowned.

"Susan called, but I didn't tell her anything." The Pine Basin operator's voice was quick and eager.

"What did she want?"

"She wanted Kelly Maynard's phone number."

"Damn." It was beginning.

"Do you want me to contact Marilyn?"

"No. If need be I'll contact her. Thank you for a job well done."

"That's what you've been paying me for all of these years."

* * * *

From the very beginning, Mary took over. By eight o'clock, she had prepared coffee in three large percolators she had borrowed from her friends. She had also managed to gather close to fifty folding chairs. Jeff and Susan were in the process of transforming their living room into a small auditorium where all the chairs, placed in neat rows, faced the fireplace.

At 9:43, the first people arrived, two housewives who had seen the interview. Shortly after that their neighbors came, followed by some more strangers and finally some of Susan's students. By 10:00 a.m., the living room was crammed with people. In spite of the anxiety gnawing at her, Susan tried to make everyone feel welcome by circulating and serving coffee to as many people as she could.

She walked through the crowd, the smallest of the three percolators in her hands. "Coffee, anyone?" she asked to no one in particular.

"Mrs. Haynes." Susan turned to face Lisa Biro, senior class president, varsity cheerleader, and a former student. "I'm so sorry," Lisa said and threw her arms around her ex-teacher.

As Susan hugged Lisa, her eyes locked in on a matronly-looking woman who was leaning against the bookcase. Her eyes, cold and hard, made Susan shiver. Her folded arms rested in front of her, and her face wore a frown.

"I remember seeing your son at school," Lisa said. "He was so cute. I mean, is...is cute." Susan returned her attention to Lisa, but not before she glanced at the unusual stranger in her living room. "I think it's just awful," Lisa continued, "just awful."

"Thank you, Lisa."

The doorbell rang again and Mary opened the door. The television crew, carrying all of their equipment, stepped inside. Through the crowded room Susan found Jeff. He seemed happy that they were going to have live coverage.

"Thank you for coming and for your concern," Susan told her student, even though her attention remained on the sour-looking lady. Susan wondered what had prompted her to come. She looked at Lisa. "Shouldn't you be at school?"

"Mr. Hensley is listing our absences as school related."

Susan nodded and made a mental note to call the principal and thank him. "That's very nice of him. Just make sure you repay him by going straight to school after this is over."

Lisa frowned. "Yeah, okay," she said. She spotted Donald, the varsity football captain. "Oh, look! There's Donald." With a big, wide, coquettish smile she walked over to him.

"Youth," Susan said to herself, then prayed that Timmy would be with her when he was a teenager. She wanted the chance to guide her son through the difficult teenage years.

Susan felt someone put an arm around her. She turned to face Jeff.

"Susan," he said, "I know it's still early, but I think we better get started. We're running out of space."

Susan nodded and signaled for Mary to join them by the fireplace. On their way, Jeff stopped to talk to his boss, Michael Ruble. "Hey, I'm sorry about missing work," he said, shaking Michael's hand.

"We miss you and we need you at the office," Michael said. "I never realized how much easier my day goes because you're there. But right now, your family needs you. Take as long as you want." He nodded at Susan.

Jeff patted Michael's arm. "Thanks. We appreciate that."

When they were out of hearing range, Susan said, "He's a nice man. Everyone is being so nice." She looked back at Michael. He was busy talking to her ex-student. "Is this going to mess up your chances for that promotion you've been working so hard to get?"

Jeff shrugged. "It doesn't matter. All I want is to get Timmy back."

By now they had reached the front of the living room. Jeff took out the crude map he had drawn on a poster board and stood it on end in front of the television. Quickly, the room grew quiet.

"First of all we want to thank each and every one of you for showing up," Jeff said. "You have no idea how deeply moved Susan and I are." He pointed to the map of the Fort Worth/Dallas metroplex. "I have here a map of our area," he explained. "As you noticed I have divided it into several sections. Area one is the area around the daycare center, then the rest of the areas work outward. I made sure it included all the transportation centers, especially the airports. What we are hoping to do is to place posters in as many places as we can."

Jeff reached for the pile of posters resting by his feet, picked up one and showed it to everyone. Written on the top in large, black, block letters were the words: HAVE YOU SEEN THIS BOY? Below that was a fairly current picture of Timmy. Under his picture in smaller letters, but still large enough to be seen from a distance, was his name. Underneath that, it read: Last seen April 11. It was followed by the police's phone number and Timmy's description.

"Which area you cover depends on where you work or live," Jeff continued. "If you cover areas one through four, come see me. Susan will take areas five, six, and seven." He pointed at Mary.

"This lady next to me, Mary, will take areas eight through ten." He paused for a moment, waiting for questions or comments. Seeing the hesitation on some people's faces, he asked, "Before we start assigning areas, does anyone have questions?"

Michael slowly stood up and cleared his throat. "The guys at the bank—we managed to put together a little money." He waved the check in front of him. "This is a certified check for ten thousand dollars, payable to whoever leads us to Timmy."

Instantly the room filled with thunderous noise. People were cheering, hugging one another, congratulating Susan and Jeff. Susan's expectations soared and the instant she closed her eyes, she could clearly see Timmy playing with his favorite toys. G. I. Joe soldiers fought their battles on top of their kitchen table. Lego castles and Lego people occupied most of the living room floor. The memory caused a shuddering spasm to rack her body.

She swallowed hard and noticed the grumpy-looking lady she had spotted earlier moving toward them.

"I have a question," she said.

Jeff nodded only once. "Go ahead."

"You ask us to help you, so we came. But I think you owe these people the truth."

"The truth?" Susan felt intimidated by her domineering ways. She reminds me of someone, Susan thought. Who?

Mother? No. Or maybe yes. Maybe someone like Mother.

Strong and powerful. Forever staring at me with accusing eyes. Why? What have I done?

"Well, will you?"

The question pulled Susan back to the present.

"What?" Susan stared straight into the camera lens which was focused on her. Now she wished they had never come.

"Can you tell us how Timmy really disappeared?"

"I went to pick him up at the daycare center and he was gone."

"That seems awfully irresponsible of the daycare." A murmur of agreement generated throughout the crowd. "Unless, of course, he had been properly signed out."

Susan glanced at Jeff and noticed a frown of worry form on his forehead.

"Is that what happened?" the woman insisted.

The crowd grew quiet. Susan felt their eyes piercing her.

Jeff reached for Susan's hand and stood protectively in front of her. "A woman who strongly resembles my wife picked Timmy up."

"Oh?" The woman cocked her head. "Does your wife have an identical twin? She must, you know, if her own son fails to notice any difference." She turned to glare at Susan. "Well? Do you have a twin?"

Dr. Orr's words clearly reverberated in Susan's mind. "Susan, I wasn't able to learn much when I visited Pine Basin, but what I did find out was that both of your parents are dead, and you have no brothers or sisters. You're all alone."

You're all alone...

"Answer me!"

Startled out of her thoughts, Susan quickly said, "There is no twin."

The woman shook her head. "I don't understand. How can the daycare personnel and Timmy not know you?"

Jeff glared at her. "I want you out of my house. Who the hell do you think you are? You come into our house and accuse my wife-accuse us...Get out!"

She stared at Jeff and refused to move, like a

plant growing roots. "Isn't it true, Mrs. Haynes, that everyone—including the children—at the daycare center insist that it was you who picked Timmy up?" Her eyes drifted toward Susan.

A small murmur of astonishment broke throughout the crowd.

"And isn't it also true," the woman continued, "that you are under psychiatric care?"

As though in unison, Susan saw the crowd's face pinch in alarm.

"Get out!" Jeff yelled. He turned to face the crowd. "What she said is not true. Several years ago, my wife was seeing a psychiatrist for completely different reasons."

"That reason, Mr. Haynes, isn't it that she has no recollection of her past? Isn't it true that your wife is a woman with a hidden past? And isn't it true that she just recently started seeing her psychiatrist again?"

Susan felt Jeff's hand tighten around hers. "Her past has nothing to do with Timmy's disappearance."

"Let's hope not," she said. "But I for one would like to know just exactly what it is that Mrs. Haynes is trying to hide. I think she knows, but she doesn't want us to find out. It's just a game she's playing. Am I right, Mrs. Haynes?" She pointed an accusing finger at her. The woman's small, beady eyes became pin points of hatred.

The same type of hatred Susan had seen before. An image splashed before her eyes.

Blood.

There was blood on her hands, her dress, even on her face. As in a trance, Susan looked around. There was Death.

Susan screamed and shrunk back even further away from the people, toward the safety of the corner.

"What is it, Mrs. Haynes?"

"Blood. All over me. On my hands, my dress. Blood. Oh, God. Blood." She plastered her hands to her face.

"Whose blood, Mrs. Haynes?"

The prevailing quiet, the horror on the crowd's faces—these reminded Susan she was here in her living room. What had that lady said? What had she said? "Could you repeat that?" she asked.

"Tell us about the blood."

Blood?

What blood? Oh my God, blood! "It...it doesn't mean anything. I just remembered...when I was young, I...I was playing...and I cut myself."

"Cut yourself?" the woman asked suspiciously.

"Yes, that's it. I...I was playing and I cut myself." Even to her own ears, the explanation sounded contrived. Where had the blood come from? "It was just a simple cut."

"Are you sure, Mrs. Haynes?"

Susan nodded, but she kept her eyes glued to the floor. She couldn't look at the people, at Jeff, yet she knew this woman was gloating in victory.

"I just wonder, Mrs. Haynes, what has become of Timmy." She paused long enough to give her statement the necessary dramatic effect. "I've changed my mind," she said. "I don't want to help you anymore." She turned to look at Jeff. "I think I'll leave now."

Throughout the entire incident the camera had been rolling and now Pat shoved a microphone under Susan's nose. "What comments do you have?" she asked.

"I love Timmy," Susan answered. "I would never hurt him."

Some of the people—neighbors, acquaintances, and students—exchanged knowing looks. One nodded, stood up and left. Another one followed, then a third, until a group did likewise. This continued until the room was practically empty.

"Hey, you can't leave them," Mary yelled. "They need you." More people continued to walk out. Some gave Jeff a sympathetic pat on the back, but most just walked out.

Michael walked over to Jeff. "Under the circumstances, Jeff, I'm afraid I'm going to have to withdraw the offer."

There was a wild look in Jeff's face. "Michael, you can't do that."

Michael placed a hand on Jeff's shoulders. "Jeff, you're a bright man, and you know I've had my eye on you for that vice-president opening." He squeezed Jeff's shoulder and removed his hand. "Our new vice-president must be someone who is enterprising, ambitious, and smart. And something else—something much more important. Do you know what that is?"

Jeff shook his head.

"He must be an excellent judge of character." He pointed his finger at Jeff. "And you, Jeff, are an excellent judge." He paused for a second. "Now, how do you suppose our customers will react if they learn that I've used their money on what may turn out to be..." He glanced in Susan's direction. "Well, I'm sure you understand." He smiled awkwardly and left.

The same room which was alive with people only a few minutes ago now stood almost deserted. There remained a solitary figure still sitting in the back row. "I warned you," he said. It was Detective Bronson.

"Who was she?" Jeff asked.

"A bitch," Bronson answered. "Her name is Dee Dee Scripto and her husband is one of our detectives, which explains where she got her informa-tion." He stood up and straightened his shirt. "I can't blame her though."

"Meaning?" Jeff asked.

"To be one hundred per cent truthful, the con-sensus at the police station is that Susan is guilty."

"And what do you think?" Susan asked.

"Me?" He scratched his chin. "I think you're innocent."

Susan let out a sigh of relief. "I am," she said. "Thanks for the vote of confidence."

"Don't mention it," he answered. "I could be wrong."

"Is that what you really think?" Susan asked.

"Let's just say that all logic—all evidence—points to you. It all fits too neatly, and that's why I'm ap-proaching this with an open mind." He tapped his forehead, as though he had forgotten something. "Be prepared for the worst," he said. "The cameras were here and they taped everything."

"You don't really think they'll air it, do you?" Jeff asked.

"Oh, they'll air it, all right," Bronson said. "They'll doctor it up a bit—make it seem as if they're showing only the facts. After all, they don't want any lawsuits over this." He shrugged. "I best be going." After a pause, he added, "Oh, if it makes you feel any better, Eric might lose his job over his wife's big mouth. This isn't the first time that this has happened, and he has been warned before, and of course, you have a nice slander lawsuit in your hands—if that sort of stuff interests you."

"I don't care what they think about me," Susan said. "All I want to do is find my Timmy."

"Right," Bronson said as he pointed his index finger at her. "Me and you—we need to talk about that blood."

Chapter Fourteen

As Bronson was walking out the front door, Jeff was briskly heading for the back door. He had to get away, for just a few minutes. A few hours. A few days.

He knew Susan could never—not even under the most strenuous of situations—harm Timmy. But that was the Susan he knew. Who was the person who had lived in Susan's body for the first eighteen years of her life? Was she capable of harming Timmy?

Just above Jeff's head, he heard a chirping sound. He looked up in time to see a bird building its nest in the blooming tree. Spring was finally here. Where was the hope and the love it was suppose to bring?

Disgustedly he went back inside. He left the back door open so that the sun's rays could filter into the kitchen.

Only the day before yesterday the three of them had sat around the kitchen table, each content with their lives. Timmy had been looking forward to his birthday. "Mommy, can we go the store today and look for my racing car set?" Timmy asked as he stabbed his egg, breaking the yolk.

"I don't know, honey," Susan said rubbing her

temples. Her head was beginning to pound.

"Oh, please. My birthday—"

"Young man, your mother said she didn't know. Now that's the end of that." Jeff threw Timmy a warning look and Timmy shrunk back into his seat. "Mommy's sick, so let's be good. Okay, tiger?"

A worried frown formed on Timmy's forehead. "Poor Mommy. I'm sorry for you," he said as he stared at his mother. He held his fork so that its tines rested on top of his forgotten egg.

"I'm okay," Susan said. "It's just a small headache." She forced herself to finish the toast which she had just smothered with grape jelly.

"I can kiss it and make it better," Timmy said. "It works when you do it."

Susan looked up at him and smiled. Her eyes said, "I love you, Timmy."

"For real," he said as he shoveled a mouthful of egg.

Jeff and Susan exchanged looks. Susan's eyes twinkled and they both laughed.

A hollow pocket of longing for the old times settled in Jeff's stomach. He sighed and returned to the living room just in time to see Mary leave.

"She went to go get her car keys," Susan said. She was sitting at the edge of the couch, her hands clasped together. Her chin was resting on her chest. She spoke without looking up. "She figures that the three of us could go put up the posters."

"I suppose we'll have to." Even though he hadn't meant to, his voice came out sounding harsh. He knew Susan wanted to be held, but he just couldn't bring himself to do it. "If a stranger picked Timmy up," he said, "how did she know you had a headache?"

"If?" Susan said.

Jeff ignored her comment. He continued, "Why

did Timmy willingly go with her? How could he not recognize you?"

"I don't know," she whispered. She started shaking. "God only knows how much I wish I knew."

As Jeff stared at his wife, a giant wave of compassion enveloped him. He knelt down beside her and gently took her in his arms. "Don't shake like that, honey. I was just thinking aloud. These are questions we are going to have to account for to the reporters and the police. But I love you, Susan. I'll stand by you."

Susan found solace in his embrace. "I know, Jeff. I just wish I had the answer. I wish I could explain the shoes."

"The shoes?" He pushed her away and stared at her. "What shoes?"

"When I got out of bed before picking Timmy up at the daycare, I reached for my shoes."

"Yeah? So?"

"My slippers weren't there by the bed." She breathed hard and through her mouth. She was constantly fighting for control of her emotions.

Jeff grabbed her by her shoulders. "What are you trying to say?" He released her.

"I always wear my slippers around the house. You know that."

"Get to the point."

"That afternoon when I got out of bed, my slippers were in the closet, and my tennis shoes were by the bed."

"Oh, God, Susan." Jeff ran his fingers through his hair. "Oh, God."

* * * *

It was past eight o'clock when Jeff returned home. He felt slightly drunk, having downed several beers at a nearby bar. He had expected to find Susan waiting for him, but either she was still hanging up posters or she was over at Mary's. Either way, he didn't care, and was glad he had the house all to himself. He would get to bed—God knew he was tired enough—and hopefully, by the time Susan got home, he'd be fast asleep.

It wouldn't be like before. On those rare moments when he went to sleep before Susan, she'd come—regardless of how long he'd been asleep—and snuggle next to him. Then she would kiss him on the lips. Jeff would groan, and she'd kiss the tip of his nose. Slowly, Jeff would open his eyes and pretend he thought it was morning. "It's that time already?" He'd feign a sleepy voice. Susan would nod and he would reach out and grab her.

Sometimes he'd look forward so much to the game that he'd hurry through his nightly chores just to make sure he'd get to bed before Susan.

Jeff wondered if he would ever want to play the game again.

Chapter Fifteen

It was past eight-thirty when Mary pulled up in front of Susan's house and let her out.

"Thanks for your help," Susan said as she leaned over to hug her friend.

"Are you going to be all right?" A worried frown formed on Mary's face.

Susan shrugged. "I'm okay. It's Timmy I'm concerned about."

"I know."

Susan reached for the door handle and began to open the door.

"Susan, are you going to watch the news tonight? Would you like me to come over and stay with you?"

"Jeff's home," Susan said as she glanced at the house, "but thanks for offering."

* * * *

Mary folded her arms in front of her and stared at the phone. The news would be on in less than half an hour. If Marilyn listened to the news...

Mary felt a tremor ignite deep within her. Surely this particular news would be covered only locally. It wouldn't be aired in Pine Basin. Still.

Mary bit her lip and once again glared at the phone. The adage "an ounce of prevention..." came to her. She quickly picked up the phone and began to dial. Soon she was connected with the Pine Basin operator. "Carla, it's me, Mary. Something's happened over here in Dallas which might upset Marilyn. If you hear anything, I want you to immediately call me."

"Of course I will." There was a slight pause. "Whatever it is, I hope it's not serious. Marilyn was just raving about her trip to Dallas. She just absolutely loved being over there with you."

"It was nice having her, although she hardly visited with me."

"I know. She told me about Susan's little boy."

Mary felt her muscles tense. "Oh? What did she say?" She tried to make her voice sound normal.

"Just how much she enjoyed being with him and how she spent every available minute with him. Did anything happen to the little boy? God, I hope not!"

"No, Carla, everything is okay, but if you hear anything unusual, call me immediately."

"Sure thing, but how will I know that what I heard is unusual?"

"Don't worry about it. You'll know."

"I see." The operator's voice sounded disappointed.

Mary hung up and turned on the television. The news was about to begin.

Chapter Sixteen

Susan sat in the dining room, a cold, full cup of coffee resting by the Dallas Morning News in front of her. She stared at the headline with the same fascination that a rat must feel when lured by a cobra. Unable to stop herself, Susan once more mouthed the headline: "WOMAN WITH NO PAST SURROUNDED BY MYSTERY."

She read the article and re-read it, each time hoping that she had misinterpreted it—that it really didn't make her seem to be the number one suspect. But she had talked about blood, and there were the headaches, and Timmy had willingly left with "Mommy." No doubt about it. The newspaper piece, in presenting only the facts, made her look guilty.

The article had of course also introduced the other side. There were many quotes from her colleagues—teachers, administrators, and even some students. They all claimed she was an excellent teacher, a caring person, and above all, "normal." They were all shocked at the accusations.

Susan let the paper drop to the floor as she stared at the wall directly in front of her. I love you, Timmy, she thought. Mommy wouldn't hurt you.

She covered her face with her hands, but, although her insides were being torn apart, she didn't cry. She had reached the point beyond tears. She felt a strong hand squeeze her shoulder.

"Susan, we've got to be strong."

She looked up. Even though Jeff's eyes were narrow slits filled with pity, his lips were curved up into a smile. He pulled up a chair beside her.

"Oh, Jeff, where's Timmy?"

Jeff shook his head and wet his lips.He still hadn't seen the newspaper, and Susan knew what it would do to him, how it would widen the crevice that had been growing between them, but she also knew that she had no choice but to hand him the paper.

"Oh, no," Jeff said as he read the headline. His complexion paled as he read the article. After he finished, he folded the newspaper and placed it on top of the dining table. "Susan, we need to talk."

Susan nodded. "Go ahead," she said.

"Did you hurt Timmy?"

Susan's world crumbled around her. She wanted to scream NO. She knew he'd be satisfied, but there were so many unanswered questions in her mind. She looked down.

Jeff's eyes turned with sudden fury. "Susan, don't ignore me. I'm trying to reach out to you. I'm trying to understand. Be fair. I can't help you if you insist on shutting me out. For my own peace of mind, I have to know. Did you hurt Timmy?"

His powerful words were a dagger in Susan's heart. She told him what he wanted to hear. "No, Jeff. I did not hurt Timmy."

"How do you know? Do you actually remember not doing it, or do you just think you didn't do it? How much do you remember of Monday?"

"I remember sending you all off, then going back to sleep and not waking until past four."

"You don't think it's unusual that after spending an entire night in bed you could sleep all day too?"

Susan shrugged.

"That's not good enough. I need explanations. Why would Miss Cortez—who's always been very nice to us—all of a sudden want to hurt us? She knows you—God we've been taking Timmy there since he was a baby—and suddenly she doesn't recognize you? It doesn't make sense."

"I know that, Jeff. I know that."

He eyed her. In a tone laced with bitterness, he continued, "Can you at least explain how that little girl at the daycare knew you had a headache on that particular day?"

"That woman who picked Timmy up kept hurrying him because she had a headache. Jenny overheard and that's how she knew."

"And how did this woman know about your headache?"

"Maybe she had a headache."

"Susan, you can't possibly believe that. The coincidence is too hard to swallow." He wore the mask of a desperate man. "You can't really expect me to believe that, can you?"

"I can't tell you what to believe, Jeff. All I know is that I didn't hurt Timmy. Don't ask me how I know that. I can't explain it, nor can I answer your questions. But I am asking you to please have faith in me. Can you do that?"

For a long time, Jeff studied Susan. Finally he said, "I can try. That's all I can promise you." He stood up. "I just wish you hadn't told me about those damn shoes."

Jeff's comment severed Susan's last ounce of strength. She felt like a raggedy doll, ready to collapse. Damn you, she thought. She would not give

him the satisfaction of showing him her weakness.
She sat perfectly still.

Jeff began to walk out of the kitchen then stopped.
Without turning around he said, "I'm sorry, Susan, but
I have to find the truth."

Chapter Seventeen

Mary awoke from a night plagued with troubled sleep. Even though it was just barely four-thirty in the morning, she knew she wouldn't return to sleep. Now she wished she hadn't told her boss that she wasn't going to work today. She could conceivably be at work by six-thirty and catch up with some of the paper work. Instead, she would have to stay home so she could help Jeff and Susan put up some more posters.

Mary sighed and forced herself to remain in bed. A little over an hour later she heard the thump of the newspaper. She put on her robe, prepared a cup of coffee, and sat down to read the newspaper.

"Oh, no!" she said when she saw the headline. A sinking sensation hit her in the bottom of her stomach when she noticed that it was a UPI story. Chances were that the article would also be featured in the Pine Basin Gazette. Marilyn would surely read it, and then—

The ringing of the phone startled Mary. She picked it up on the second ring.

"Mary?"

She sucked in her breath. It was David, her ex-husband.

"Mary, is that you?"

"Yes."

"Have you seen the paper?" he asked.

Like a fool, Mary nodded.

"Mary, are you there?"

"Yes, I've seen it."

"I can't believe Susan would do anything like that."

No answer.

He continued, "I see. Then I was right. What are you doing about it?"

"I'm helping Susan and Jeff."

"Helping? How?"

"In just a couple of hours we're going to go put up some posters of Timmy's picture."

"That's not the kind of help they need from you. You need to—"

"I know. I know," Mary desperately answered.

"Then do something about it, because if you ignore it, I'll take care of it. And believe me, Mary, I'll take care of it by going straight to the police. Tomorrow, I'll call back. See what you can do by then." David slammed the phone down and Mary cringed.

What now? If she didn't do anything about it, that bastard would go to the police. There was no doubt in her mind.

What Mary needed to do was go to work. There, she would distance herself from the problem, and she'd be able to reason it out. Later, she'd call Susan and tell her that her boss had called very early, pleading with her to come to work. Mary had no choice but to go.

Chapter Eighteen

Susan was about to dial Mary's phone number when her doorbell rang.

"Susan, hi," Bronson said as he let himself in. "I need your help. I got this form to fill out—there's always a form. The movies make police work look so excitin', but it's not. It's all pretty routine and filled with forms. Forms, forms, forms. Do you have any coffee?" He headed toward the kitchen. Susan followed him.

"And Jeff?" Bronson asked as he watched Susan prepare the coffee.

Susan shrugged. "Out walking, I suppose."

"That's good. Walkin' is good for you."

After she had poured two cups of coffee, they took them to the dining table and sat down. "How can I help you with your forms, Detective Bronson?"

"I was doin' real good on them until I got to this 'blood' business." He took a large gulp of coffee. "Good as ever," he said, adding more cream and sugar. "Now, about this blood."

Susan shook her head. "I'm sorry. I don't think I can help you."

"Would you mind tellin' me why you can't?"

"Every once in a while I get images—like fragments of a dream. Yesterday, I closed my eyes and I saw the blood. Nothing else."

"Nothin' else?"

Susan shook her head.

"What you need to do is concentrate. Pretend I'm this Dr. Orr character and he tells you to think about this blood. Now, can you do that? Can you concentrate on that blood?"

"I...I've tried, but—"

"No, no, Susan. Don't ever say you can't." He stood up, returned to the kitchen, opened the refrigerator, retrieved a bottle of catsup, and returned to the dining table. He set the bottle down in front of Susan. "Here. Focus on this. Think red. Close your eyes. Relax. Red."

Susan smiled.

"Now, Susan, this isn't going to work if you don't cooperate." He tapped his forehead with his open palm. "Maybe you don't wanna remember. Are you hidin' somethin' in there?"

Susan's smile faded and she straightened up. Timmy. The blood. She closed her eyes. That damn blood. Where had it come from?

* * * *

"Come on, Kelly," Susan urged. "It's no fun without you. I've been there before, remember?" The wind blew through Susan's golden hair, making her feel giddy.

"But Mom said not to go past the stream," Kelly protested.

"It's perfectly safe," Susan said, placing her hands on her hips. "Besides, how can I show you my Secret Place if you don't come with me?"

Kelly frowned, and Susan took that as a sign of her giving in.

"If you don't share my Secret Place with me, I won't let you be my best friend anymore," Susan said.

"Oh, okay," Kelly said reluctantly, but still she held back.

"Well, come on," Susan urged. She could feel the anger at Kelly's indecisiveness begin to build in the pit of her stomach. "Hurry!"

"What about her?" She pointed with her head.

"She can come. She always does," Susan said.

"Yeah, but then it won't be our secret place," Kelly protested.

"Oh, yes, it will. She won't tell anybody." Susan threw back her head and laughed. "You never will, will you?"

* * * *

"You never will, will you?"

"You never will, will you?"

"YOU NEVER WILL, WILL YOU?"

"...WILL YOU?"

Susan threw her hands over her ears and screamed, "No! I never will." Her body shook with giant sobs. "I never will."

"Susan. Susan!" Bronson gently tapped her shoulder.

Startled, Susan looked up. "I...I can't," she sobbed. "I promised not to."

"Some promises are made in childish haste and are not meant to be kept. Now, go on."

Susan massaged the increasing pounding sensation inside her head. "It's no good. Once these headaches come, I can't do anything at all."

"But you didn't get to the blood part," Bronson protested.

They sat there quietly, Susan constantly frowning with the irritating pain which promised to ruin another day.

"Are you aware that there were three of you?" Bronson asked.

"What?"

"See, right here in my notes." Bronson pointed to his spiral notebook. "It says here, 'What about her?' Who was that third member of your group?"

The question disturbed Susan enough to send a bolt of pain shooting to the back of her skull, creating a green and yellow speckled mist before her eyes. Still, she tried to put a handle on what it was that lurked in the bottom drawer of her mind.

She saw...a shadow. The same shadow Kelly's mother had stared at with such distaste. Who was this shadow? Someone unimportant. Someone insignificant. A tag-along. But who?

Her headache hit her with such brutal force that it caused her vision to blur and her teeth to ache. "I...don't know," she said.

Bronson stood up. "You head toward that pharmacy of yours in the bathroom. Take whatever helps you the most and I'll be back." He snapped his notebook shut. "You see, Susan, right now I have no choice but to believe that the blood you remembered was Timmy's. And that's what I'm goin' to put in my form, in triplicate."

Chapter Nineteen

For a little over an hour, Susan slept. When she awoke, she was thankful that most of her headache was gone. She had put Jeff through a lot, and she would make it up to him by fixing his favorite super, spaghetti with her special meatballs. Susan went into the kitchen, took some ground beef out of the freezer and put it in the microwave. She was about to punch in the time when the jangling of the phone sent her rushing to answer it. "Hello?"

There was a pause. A long pause.

"Hello!" Susan repeated. "Who's this?" Her first thoughts were of Timmy. What if he was calling and he was so scared he couldn't talk? She hadn't meant to sound so ugly. Susan forced her voice to sound peaceful and calm. "Timmy? Is that you, dear?" She bit her tongue while she waited for the answer.

Seconds later, it came. "You call yourself a good woman, but you're nothing but a bitch." The male voice sounded rough and obviously disguised. "Why, you're nothing but a fucking child killer!"

Something about the way he spoke, the way he expressed himself. It must be Billy. Billy Hawkings, Susan thought. Two months ago, Susan had caught him passing some joints in her class, and she had turned him in to the principal. Billy was then placed in the Alternative Program. Ever since then, he had carried a grudge against Susan.

But a grudge bad enough to hurt Timmy? Billy was only sixteen or seventeen. He couldn't possibly disguise himself as a woman, much less Susan. Or could he?

"Bitch." Then the receiver slammed down.

Susan's hand lingered on the phone. She noticed that she was shaking. She looked up and saw Jeff standing by the front door.

"Who was it?" He was pale.

"One of my students, I think." Susan told him about Billy. Jeff paid very close attention, especially when she got to the part about carrying a grudge.

"Call Bronson," he said and walked back out, his face buried in a frown.

* * * *

Detective Bronson didn't seem very concerned about Billy, although he did promise Susan that he was going to talk to him, just in case. "But I really think it was just a crank call," he said.

"That was so cruel," Susan mumbled.

"Well, you might as well get used to it, Susan. It was the first, but I'm sure it wasn't the last."

It's not fair, Susan thought, but she knew he was right. She hung up the phone and returned to the kitchen. She set the microwave to thaw and pressed in the time. She was thinking about Timmy when, once again, the ringing of the phone jarred her out of her thoughts.

"It's me," said the voice over the phone. "How are you doing?"

"Mary! I'll be ready to go put up the posters as soon as I get some stuff ready for tonight's supper."

"Susan, dear, I'm at work."

Shock, intertwined with alarm, nibbled at Susan. "At work? What are you doing there? I thought you were going to help—"

"I was, and I still plan to. But my boss called me early this morning and practically begged me to come to work. We're so swamped, I'm not even having lunch. But maybe I can still help you after work—depending on what time I get off."

"Don't worry, Mary. Jeff and I can manage." Susan felt bitter disappointment, but Mary had already done so much for her. She couldn't ask her to do more.

"Susan?"

"Yes."

"Have you remembered anything else about Kelly?"

"I remembered a path."

There was a loud gasp. Susan imagined everyone at work was probably staring at Mary.

"Are you all right?" Susan asked.

"Yes," Mary quickly answered. "I just reached into my drawer for a paper clip and stabbed myself with a straight pin. Now, what were you saying about a path?"

"Nothing. I don't even know why I remembered that. Why can't I remember the really important things?"

"Don't push yourself. Some things are best left alone."

"But what if my past is connected to Timmy's disappearance?"

"It isn't. I told you that before. There's no possible way the two incidents are connected."

"How do you know, Mary?"

"I just know. It's a feeling, I guess."

"Mary, you yourself told me that my instincts have always been strong. You even went as far as to say that I have a considerable amount of ESP."

"I remember."

"Well, my feelings tell me that Timmy's disappearance is connected to my past. And for Timmy's sake, I'll do my darnedest to remember."

"Susan, please don't." Mary's voice sounded far away, as though she was preoccupied.

"Why not?"

There was a slight hesitation. Then, "I'm afraid for you. Remember what Dr. Orr said."

"Well, damn Dr. Orr."

Chapter Twenty

It had been over half an hour since Jeff returned home from his walk. Susan hoped that they could talk, but instead he headed for their bedroom.

Susan understood that Jeff needed to be alone, but enough was enough. If they were to reach the people, then they needed to get out and continue to put up posters throughout the Dallas/Fort Worth metroplex.

Susan headed for the bedroom and bumped into Jeff in the hallway. He was wearing his light beige suit and the brown tie—the one Timmy had given him for Christmas. Susan had tried to discourage Timmy from buying that one because she knew Jeff wouldn't like it. But Timmy had insisted. Up until today that tie had remained in Jeff's drawer. Susan wondered why he was so dressed up.

"I decided to go to work," he said as though reading her thoughts. He looked down at the floor, avoiding Susan's eyes.

"But, Jeff, the posters," she protested.

He shrugged. "I don't think it'll make much difference."

"Jeff, how can you say that?"

"Look, the reason for those posters is so people can see Timmy's face and remember it. Well, his face and yours has been plastered in every goddamned newspaper in the nation. It's publicity we wanted, it's publicity we got. Thanks to you and your...your hidden past."

His words were a blade ripping through Susan's soul. "That's not fair," she said.

"Fair? Do you think what's happened to Timmy is fair? It's not his fault that you...you..." He threw his arms up in the air, then covered his eyes.

"You think I hurt him, don't you?" Even as she spoke, she found it hard to believe that she had to ask him this. "Don't you?" she repeated.

Jeff looked down and shrugged. The silence that followed wasn't the comfortable silence they had grown accustomed to, but a silence which divided them and left Susan feeling cold and alone. She realized that not only had she lost Timmy, she was also losing Jeff.

"Susan." Jeff's voice sounded dry. He cleared his throat. "I...I need time. I'm trying to understand. I..." He ran his fingers through his hair. He sighed and took a few steps forward. "I'm already late for work," he said. As he walked past Susan, he squeezed her shoulder.

* * * *

Susan stared at the stack of Timmy posters. Even if everyone gives up, I won't, she told herself. She fixed her hair, stepped into the closet, and reached for her tennis shoes. She didn't find them. Instead, she saw her slippers. Her eyes dropped down to her feet. She was wearing her tennis shoes—not her slippers—inside the house.

Ripples of hope shot through her veins. This morning she had wanted to get a very early start with the posters. She had deliberately put on her tennis shoes. Was that what happened Monday morning? She flopped down on the bed. She hadn't gone out Monday. Why were the shoes there? Then she remembered. Sunday night—the night before Timmy disappeared—she had decided to jog, hoping that it would unknot her tense muscles.

It had worked, but by the time she got back, she felt excessively worn-out. She had taken off her shoes, flopped down on the bed and immediately fallen asleep. The next morning she had awakened with such a tremendous headache that she remained in bed.

A complex wave of relief and anxiety struck Susan with such ferocity that she groaned out loud and grabbed her forehead. Timmy. Timmy, I didn't hurt you. But where are you, my son? Are you all right?Are you alive?

* * * *

Mary sat staring at the day's work spread in front of her.

"Hey, Mary, work isn't going to get done like that."

Startled, Mary looked up and saw her boss Mr. Stranton glaring at her. He was a tall, gaunt man with two raisins for eyes.

"I'm sorry," she said, picking up the pile of letters which needed to be filed. "I just have other things on my mind."

"Then go home and handle your problems over there." He folded his arms in front of him.

She knew he was being sarcastic, but she decided to take him at his word. "I think I will." Mary dropped the pile of letters back on her desk, opened the bottom drawer, and retrieved her purse. "Thank you for your understanding."

As she brushed past him, she saw that Mr. Stranton was standing staring at her with wide, unblinking eyes and a wide-open mouth. Had Mary not been so furious, she probably would have smiled.

But he's right, Mary thought as she backed her car out of the company's enclosed parking lot. I do need to settle this, and a phone call to Pine Basin will not suffice.

She stopped at a red light and drummed her fingers against the steering wheel while she waited for the light to turn green. She would have to fly to Pine Basin, unannounced, and pop in on Marilyn. Someone behind her honked and Mary realized the light had turned green. As soon as she got home she would call work—if she still had a job— and tell them she'd have to be out tomorrow. She would use helping Susan as an excuse.

She drove off, feeling better, knowing that one way or the other, by tomorrow she would have the answer.

Chapter Twenty-One

"No, you cannot put that poster in my restaurant," the owner said. She was a large woman with so much extra bulk that she looked like an overstuffed potato sack. "People who come here want to forget about the world and its problems. Your poster would only remind them that it's an ugly world outside."

"But if one of your customers—"

"Sorry," the owner interrupted and abruptly turned away.

People can be so cruel, Susan thought as she turned to leave. There must be a way. Susan bit her lip, trying to think of an alternative. Maybe she could put the poster outside the restaurant.

Susan turned to follow the owner into the kitchen. She walked into the middle of a conversation. "...killed her own kid, you know." The owner had her back to Susan and she was talking to another woman, apparently the cook. "No way was I going to let that lying bitch put some posters up."

Susan held her head up high and stormed out, feeling everyone's eyes following her. Once outside, the gentle breeze seemed to help her burning eyes.

She tried other restaurants, some stores, malls, and public buildings. Each time she came out, she knew people were talking about her, accusing her. Afterwards, Susan placed the posters on park benches, trees, telephone poles—any place she could think of. Exhausted, she headed home.

As she turned down Washington Avenue, less than a mile away from home, she eased off the gas pedal, very much aware that she didn't want to go home. She didn't want to face Jeff. Jeff, with his accusing eyes.

The realization frightened her. Jeff was her pillar of strength. She had always found comfort, love, and understanding in Jeff. But not any longer. Where once her marriage was strong and solid, it was now on shaky ground. She knew it was a matter of time before her marriage disintegrated completely.

Hollow pockets of emptiness invaded her soul. She couldn't think of Jeff. It was Timmy she needed to concentrate on.

She considered stopping at the store, buying grape Pop Tarts—Timmy's favorite. She was out of them and she knew Timmy would want some when he got home. She could hear his voice just as clear as if he was sitting next to her. "I ate everything, Mommy. Now can I have my pa-tars? Huh, Mommy?" His eyes would open wide with anticipation.

Susan's vision blurred. Yes, sweetheart, you can have your Pop Tarts. As soon as you come home, I'll fill you up with Pop Tarts. Just please come home.

Without realizing it, she reached her house. She sat in her drive, staring at its vast emptiness. It was such a big, lonely place. She took the keys out of the ignition, and once inside, she headed straight for the refrigerator, where she poured herself a glass of apple wine.

Longing for a friendly voice, she dialed Mary's number. She let the phone ring for a long time before hanging up. Even Mary is avoiding me now.

She flopped down on the couch and stared at the wall. After a while, the phone rang. Susan ran to answer it and picked it up on the third ring. "Hello?"

"Hi ya, Susan. How ya doing?" That was Detective Bronson. Susan recognized his gentle yet powerful voice. "We might have our first lead."

Susan held her breath. "Who...what..."

"You know Julie Ward from Happy Child Daycare?"

"Yes, of course." Susan's insides tightened.

"We've run a routine check on each of the employees. Now we don't have anything yet, so don't go getting scared or anything. But a few days back we found that Miss Ward has a record for child molesting."

"Oh, God!"

"Now, Susan, like I said, we don't know that she's done anything. We've had her under surveillance and it seems like we might be climbing up the wrong tree. But either way, we're bringing her in for questioning."

"I'll be right there."

"No, you won't. I got enough problems over here without you coming over. I'll call you if we get anything. I'll call you even if we don't get anything."

He was right. There was nothing Susan could do over there. But at least now she had hope. It all made sense. Of course someone at the daycare center had to have been involved. Susan had been very naive not to have seen it before. That explained everything.

But if this was true then that meant that...that... The realization hit Susan with such a sudden impact that it made her feel as if she was falling from a tall building. But she never quite reached the bottom. She kept falling.

Falling.

What has she done to my Timmy? Is he at this moment calling out to me? Is he crying? Or is he dead and buried—a look of horror etched on his face for eternity?

"Timmy!" Susan screeched at the top of her lungs.

She picked up the first object she could find—an encyclopedia—and hurled it across the room. It went crashing against the window pane. She picked up the lamp and smashed it against the floor. Then another book, a vase, a souvenir they had picked up when they took Timmy to Sea World last year. This one crushed against the fireplace, knocking Timmy's picture from the mantle. It tumbled down, cracking the glass.

Susan ran over to it. "Oh, Timmy, I'm sorry, honey." She picked up the broken picture and cradled it in her arms. "I'm so sorry, Timmy. Mommy didn't mean to."

"Didn't mean to what?" said a harsh voice behind her.

Startled, Susan turned. It was Jeff. He took a menacing step forward. "Didn't mean to what?" Susan could see the veins in his neck pulsating with anger.

"Oh, Jeff," she sobbed. "They found her."

There was confusion in his eyes. "What?"

"Julie—Julie what's her name?—from the daycare center. The police got her. Oh, Jeff." Susan tried not to cry. "She's got a record for child molestation."

Immediately his features softened, as if he had been struck by a wave of shame. He sat shaking his head, looking down at the floor. "Oh, Susan," he mumbled, "then you didn't—" He reached out for Susan and hugged her. "I'm so sorry." He buried his face in her shoulder. "So sorry."

"Oh, Jeff, she's got our boy."

"What did the police say?" His green eyes almost looked brown and sunken, like jars filled with sorrow. "Is he all right?"

"They don't know. Detective Bronson will call us as soon as he knows something. All we can do is wait. I don't think I can do that. I've got to know if he's all right."

"I know," he said, squeezing Susan. He gently stroked her hair. "I know."

* * * *

Several times Susan started to pick up the phone to call Bronson. Each time she put it back. She paced the room, wondering why he hadn't called. Unable to wait a minute longer, she picked up the car keys.

"Put them back," Jeff said. "You'd be so angry, you'd probably blow Bronson's strategy wide open."

So they waited.

Susan suggested supper. Jeff wasn't hungry. Susan was glad. The thought of food repulsed her. They turned on the television set but within ten minutes it was back off. They listened to the radio, but changed the station several times; finally it too went off.

"Cards?" Jeff asked. Susan nodded. Jeff went over to get a deck.

Susan looked at her watch: 8:47. Why hadn't Bronson called?

Jeff returned with a deck of cards. He dealt them five cards each.

"What are we playing?" Susan asked.

He shrugged, then added, "Poker?"

Susan nodded as she stared at the cards, their denominations not really registering.

The doorbell rang. Both Jeff and Susan jumped up to answer it. Jeff opened the door and saw that Detective Bronson looked down to the floor, then up at them. He shifted his weight from one foot to the other.

"Timmy?" Susan asked, afraid to hear the answer.

"We still don't know. You see, uh, Ma'am, Sir, this thing here didn't quite turn out the way I thought it would. I can honestly tell you that I believe Ms. Ward is innocent."

His answer plucked Susan's soul out of her chest. Unable to think of anything to say, she nodded.

"But I thought you guys had something." Jeff dragged his fingers through his hair. "Now you're telling me we're right back where we started—with nothing."

"I'm sorry, Jeff. I wish I had better news. I know how you feel." He cleared his throat. "I have more to say." He looked all around him. "You know, I really think we'd be more comfortable in the living room." He walked the rest of the way in. Jeff closed the door behind them, looked at Susan, and shrugged.

Bronson, leading the way, reached the living room first, sat down on the couch, but did not lean back. "I want to know about Kelly," he said.

"And I want to know what's going on at the police station," Jeff answered.

"Truthfully?"

The question took Jeff by surprise. "Yes, of course, the truth."

"Fair enough. You pay your taxes—my salary. You got a right to know. First, we ran each of the employees at Happy Child Daycare through the T.C.I. computer."

"The what?" Susan asked.

"The Texas Crime Information computer. It gives us instant information on anyone we're looking for. That's how we found out that Ms. Ward wasn't as squeaky clean as she looked. So we watched her for a while, hoping she'd lead us to Timmy. When that failed, we brought her in. That too was a total waste. Tomorrow, we will waste more time by giving her a polygraph test."

"A what?" Susan asked.

"A lie detector test."

"What for?" Jeff's voice sounded irritated. "You said it would be a waste of time."

"Right!" Bronson answered. "But at this point, I'm buying Susan some time."

"Meaning?" Susan felt her stomach turn.

"The D.A.—that's the District Attorney—he's a very smart man, and he's got his own theory on this kidnapping. Are either of you aware that we don't need a body to arrest someone if we feel there's probable cause?"

Jeff bolted out of the couch and walked directly toward Bronson. He stood staring straight down at him. "Get to the point."

"Aha. Good suggestion. This man's got a head on his shoulder." Bronson seemed unconcerned about Jeff's threatening manner.

"Detective Bronson, do you mind if—"

"Sit down, Jeff. Sit down." Bronson patted the couch next to him. Jeff did and Bronson continued, "Now where was I? I really should be taking notes."

"You were talking about the D.A.," Susan prompted.

"Ah, yes, of course, a very fine man. Also a very determined man. Now I'm not trying to threaten you. I'm trying to tell it as it is. The D.A.— he wants me to arrest you, Ma'am, as soon as I wrap up Ms. Ward."

Susan's energy drained away. "I didn't do anything."

"That's exactly what I told the D.A." Bronson threw his arms up in the air. "But he doesn't believe me. And that's why I'm here. I wanna know all about that blood, Kelly, and our mysterious shadow."

Susan leaned back on the couch and tried to remember...

Chapter Twenty-Two

Susan ran down the path knowing full well that somewhere behind her the other girls followed, but she didn't slow her pace. If they really wanted to know about the Secret Place, then let them run and catch up.

"Wait for us," Kelly begged. "We don't know this trail like you do. We can't go that fast."

Susan smiled and increased her pace. In her haste, she almost didn't hear it. It began no louder than a breath of air traveling through the dense forest. Susan stopped for a second and listened. Were they there? Had they whispered something? Her name, perhaps?

Susan studied the trees in front of her. There. Behind that pine. Behind the bushes. That's where they were. The voices. The voices of the miners and gold diggers who traveled this path, searching for gold. Always searching, never finding. They were calling her, urging her to bring them Kelly. Now their voices rose like a vaporous cloud moving past and around Susan. The sense of excitement made her feel lightheaded. "Soon," she whispered. "Soon."

Somewhere behind her, Kelly tripped and fell. After the initial shock had worn off, Kelly got up and dusted herself off. She looked down at her skinned right knee.

Afraid she wouldn't want to go on any further, Susan turned back. "We're almost here," she encouraged.

"It doesn't matter," Kelly answered. "I'm going back."

"You don't know the way back," Susan said. "You'll get lost."

Kelly looked behind her. The dark, threatening woods surrounded her. She frowned and Susan realized that she had been right. Smiling, Susan turned around.

"Don't go," Kelly begged.

Susan headed toward the Secret Place, never stopping to check if the girls were following. She automatically assumed they would.

Suddenly, she stopped. In front of her, the trail came to an abrupt end. The cliff dropped forty or fifty feet down in a straight line. A giant ponderosa pine had long since fallen and served as a bridge between the two. On the other side of the drop, the trail continued, but no one could see it except Susan. She knew it was there.

The voices told her.

The voices of the desolate men who came this way, searching for their fortune. They were all gone now, those gold-diggers. But their souls remained, trapped in time by the beckoning mountains. They were waiting and Susan was coming. She was bringing them Kelly.

Just like she had promised.

* * * *

Fatigue enveloped Susan like thousands of tiny probing fingers. She reached out and massaged her temples with shaking hands. Her body shivered as her forehead and armpits grew moist.

Jeff sat quietly on the love seat, his arms tightly folded in front of him. His head hung low, and he stared at the floor as though his entire world would crumble if he removed his eyes from that spot.

Susan looked up at Bronson. His normally velvety dark eyes were hard and cold, like diamonds blazing with confusion. His body was rigid. "These voices you hear, Susan, what do they tell you?"

Bronson's question hit Susan like a straight shot below the heart. Surely Bronson and especially Jeff—they don't think— They must know that happened a long, long time ago. And it's over now. Isn't it?

She tried to remember. Concentrate. As she did, a spinning sensation overtook her. Susan tried to keep from grimacing as the thumping sensation volleyed between her temples. "Nothing." Why had she whispered it? Why wasn't her voice normal? She cleared her throat, hoping that would do the trick. "The voices are gone. They've been gone for a long time. I don't hear them anymore."

"How do you know?" Jeff asked.

He might as well have slapped her. She sank back into the couch, panic gripping her. "I'd know if I was hearing them, wouldn't I?"

"I bet you weren't aware of it as a child," Jeff said. His eyes were dull and lifeless, like coal. "Listening to the bits and pieces of your childhood, you seemed to be a perfectly normal child. You were loving and warm, but once you got on that trail, it was as if you were someone completely different." For a fraction of a second he looked up at her, shook his head and added, "Is it like that now, Susan?"

Susan opened her mouth to answer, but nothing came out. She didn't know what to say.

"You and Kelly," Bronson said, "were pretty good friends. No?"

Susan nodded. "I suppose so."

"What about you and the other girl?"

A vague shape formed before Susan. Who was this third member? Susan shrugged. "I don't know. I can't even remember who she is. She's more like a shadow rather than a real person."

"Why do you keep her hidden?" Bronson asked.

"You're beginning to sound like Dr. Orr," Susan answered.

"Pardon me, Ma'am. I was just thinkin' aloud. It's a bad habit of mine." Bronson stood up. "If you don't mind me saying so, Susan, I do believe you're hiding something."

"I'm not!"

"That's just it. I don't think you know that you know. But like I said, I'm just thinkin' aloud. You must excuse my outbursts. I don't even know this Dr. Orr—at least not officially. I certainly didn't mean to sound like him." He started to leave, but stopped. "Did I tell you, Susan, that I'm picking you up tomorrow at nine?" He walked toward the door.

"Wait, Detective Bronson," Susan said. "Why are you picking me up?"

"Well, you see I hate to drive. Did you ever meet a policeman who hates to drive? That's kind of strange, huh?"

"Where are you taking my wife?"

"Since Ms. Ward is taking her polygraph test tomorrow, I thought Susan should too. This way I only go there once. My partner always used to drive. But now I have no partner. Do you think, Susan, you'd like to drive? We'll still take my car."

Jeff and Susan stared at him.

"It was just a thought," he said. "I'll see you in the morning and on the way there you can tell me all about that mysterious shadow of yours. And, oh, yes, the blood. You never got to the part about the blood." He took off his glasses and chewed on the ear piece. "This friend of yours, Mary...Mary, uh..."

"Logan."

"Yeah, that's it. Did you know she started working at Belle View Mental Institute on the same day you were institutionalized?"

That was news to her. Why hadn't Mary ever mentioned it? She noticed that Bronson was studying her. "Yes, as a matter of fact, I did," Susan lied. She didn't know what he was getting at, but she didn't care for the way he always gave out tidbits of information without really saying anything. Besides, what difference did it make when Mary began?

"Right," Bronson said. He put his glasses back on and without any further delay, he walked out the door.

As the door closed, Jeff collapsed onto the couch. "Go on to bed," he said. "I'll be there in a while."

Susan nodded and breathed a sigh of relief. He wasn't going to leave her, at least not yet.

* * * *

As Susan drew the bedroom curtains closed, she noticed Mary's dark house. It was strange that Mary hadn't called. Was she, like everyone else, also doubting her?

Chapter Twenty-Three

Susan lay in bed, eyes closed, but wide awake. Her mind was a blank, asking only one question: Why? Why had Timmy disappeared? Why was her past so important. Why? WHY?

WHY?

She rolled over and saw Timmy's face, fear swimming in his eyes like bright red fish in a muddy pond. She heard his voice rising to a high shrill. "No, Mommy. No. Please. No. Nooo..."

In her hands she carried a large meat-carving knife. Its blade shone like a death star, slowly drawing her into its horrifying trap.

Her hands.

Her dress.

All smeared with blood.

She sat bolt upright, her body drenched with perspiration. She breathed through her mouth as she surveyed the surroundings.

A dresser. A bureau. Jeff peacefully sleeping beside her. It had just been a nightmare. She glanced at the alarm clock and wiped the sweat off her forehead: 6:14 a.m. There was no need trying to get back to sleep. She got dressed, made breakfast, then waited for Bronson to come. It seemed that lately she had developed a talent for doing just that: waiting.

* * * *

A few minutes past ten, Susan was strapped to a machine with a band around her chest and another one around her arm, as if the examiner was going to take her blood pressure. He was a short, plump man with coarse black hair framing an almost perfect oval face. Beady brown eyes looked over the top of his small wire-framed glasses. "Are you nervous?" he asked.

"A little."

"No need to be," he said as he strapped another band around Susan's finger tips. "All I'm going to do is ask you some simple questions and you answer yes or no. That's all." He smiled, trying to reassure Susan.

"Sounds easy," she said.

"Good. Then let's begin." He leaned over the machine as he asked, "Are you a school teacher?"

"Yes."

"Do you live in California?"

"No."

"Have you ever stolen anything in your life?"

"No, well, yes. Maybe. When I was little," Susan said.

"Please stick to yes and no answers."

"I'm sorry."

"Let's begin again," he said. "Are you a school teacher?"

"Yes."

"Do you live in California?"

"No."

"Have you ever stolen anything in your life?"

"Yes."

"Is your name Susan Haynes?"

Susan opened her mouth to answer, but for a fraction of a second she couldn't think of the answer.

"Is your name Susan Haynes?" the man repeated.

"Yes," she mumbled.

"Do you have a son?'

"Yes."

"Do you know where he is?"

"No."

"Do you hear voices?"

"No."

"Did you hurt your son?"

"No."

"Do you love him?"

"Yes."

"Did you kill your son?"

"No."

The interrogation continued. The same questions were asked. The same answers were given. After what seemed to be an eternity, the examiner played around with some knobs on the machine and unstrapped Susan. "Thank you very much," he said.

"How did I do?"

"I give 'em. The police read 'em," he said as he undid the last band. "That's my policy." He pointed to his right. "Two doors down, there's a waiting room. Detective Bronson will join you in a minute."

The room was a small area with a dull gray couch, a plain end table, and two metal folding chairs in desperate need of new paint. Susan choose the couch over the metal chairs. It looked safer, if not more comfortable.

Within five minutes, Bronson came in with two cups of coffee. "Do you take sugar and cream with yours?" he asked.

Susan nodded.

"I was afraid of that," he said. "There isn't any." He set the cup of coffee in front of her. It had cream and after Susan tasted it, she knew it had sugar. Puzzled, she looked up.

Bronson smiled and Susan smiled back.

"You're clear," he said as he sat on the couch beside her.

"It showed I was telling the truth." This was more of a statement than a question.

"The machine says you're telling the truth when you say that you didn't hurt Timmy," he said.

"You believe me now?" Susan asked.

"I never disbelieved you."

"Then why the test?"

"Once, I was wrong." He raised his index finger signifying the number one.

"Once?" Susan teased.

"Well, maybe, once too often."

Susan smiled, but even before the smile had fully bloomed, it died on her lips like a wilted flower. Bronson's icy look startled her. She knew he was studying her as one would an alien.

"Who are you?" Bronson's voice was thick with emotion.

Caught off guard, Susan couldn't think of an answer, couldn't even understand the question. His eyes seemed to scrutinize her soul. "I'm Susan," she mumbled. "Susan Haynes."

"Are you really?"

Susan giggled, like a child at a funeral. "Of course. Who else?" Her insides were waging a war, and she fought to keep control.

Bronson smirked. "I don't know who else." His voice was now gentle, the harshness gone. "But there is no evidence of any Susan McFields—that is your maiden name. Right?"

Susan nodded.

"If that is your name, then there's something drastically wrong. You see, there are no records of any kind about someone named Susan McFields. No birth records, no school records, and a social security number only after you left Belle View." He stood up and paced the room. "Do you understand what I'm saying?"

Susan nodded numbly.

"Can you explain that?"

She shook her head.

"As far as the world is concerned, you were born on the day you arrived at Belle View Mental Institute."

Susan gasped in disbelief. "I don't understand."

"I have what may possibly be two theories. Now mind you, I did say theories. I'm working on both." He spoke as though he were presenting a dissertation to his college professor. "One: you are not Susan McFields. Evidence: there isn't one shred of information which substantiates your existence prior to your admittance into the loony farm." His cheeks turned red. "Uh, excuse me. I meant to say mental institute." Once done with the apology, he quickly continued, "Evidence number two." He raised two fingers to signify the number. "The test showed you were lying when you said your name is Susan."

Susan's mind, jumbled with fragmentary thoughts and emotions, was stretched to its limits. She stood rigidly, sweat running down her back. "I am Susan. I have to be. My ancestors founded Pine Basin. I may not remember much about my youth, but I do remember growing up in Pine Basin."

"That's the fallacy of Theory Number One, which leads us to Theory Number Two. You are Susan McFields, but somebody paid through the nose to obliterate any records dealing with your history."

Susan liked this theory better even if the thought scared her. "But why would anyone want to do that?"

"I suppose they wanted to make sure that if you ever recovered your memory, there was no way to prove whatever it is you can't remember."

"But who would do that?"

"I have my theories but I never discuss theories until I am sure of them."

"But you just mentioned two theories."

"Those, my dear girl, are not theories," Bronson said with a smirk. "One of those is the truth."

Chapter Twenty-Four

As soon as Jeff arrived at work, he noticed the note on his desk. It informed him that Michael wanted to see him as soon as possible.

Jeff frowned. There was only one reason why the boss would want to see him. He was going to be let down as easily as possible. He would be informed, most regrettably, that he'd been bypassed for the promotion.

He might as well get it over with. He headed for the bank president's office and knocked on the door. "Michael?" Jeff said, sticking his head into the room. "I understand you wanted to see me."

Michael looked up from the papers he was signing. "Jeff, please sit down." He pointed to an empty chair. "I have some unpleasant news, and the only way to do this is to hand it to you straight out."

Bronson, Susan, Timmy—had they called? Jeff's heart caught in his throat. "The police—"

Michael gasped. "Oh, no, Jesus, Jeff, I'm so sorry. I never meant to..."

Jeff waved his hand. "It's my fault. All I do is think about Timmy. It's about the job, isn't it?"

Michael wiped his forehead with his open hand. "You've got to understand, Jeff, that a bank such as ours must maintain a very squeaky clean image. Now, damn it, Jeff, both you and I know that you're the man for this job. But as long as this little business concerning your wife remains unsolved..." He shrugged. "You understand, don't you?"

Jeff nodded and glanced down.

* * * *

Susan spent the rest of the day putting up Timmy's posters wherever she could. Although she expected to be home in time to fix a decent supper, it was past six before she pulled up next to Jeff's car parked in the driveway.

"Jeff?" she called out as she entered the house. She found him sitting on the couch, his hands plastered to this face. She held her breath—afraid to ask, yet needing to know. "Timmy?"

He shook his head. "No news yet."

"What's wrong, Jeff?" She reached out for him. He shrank back and Susan removed her hands.

"I'm sorry," he said. "It was an involuntary reaction."

I know, she thought. Susan sat at the opposite end of the couch. "How's work?" she asked while her insides yelled, Talk to me. Don't shut me out.

He shrugged. "I turned down the promotion," he said without looking up.

"Jeff, why? You worked so hard."

He looked at Susan, smirked and returned his eyes to the floor. "It doesn't matter."

"Yes, it does. Why did you turn it down?"

Jeff's reply was an almost imperceptible shaking of his head.

"I see," Susan said, standing up. "I'm sorry." She walked out.

A shroud of sorrow enveloped her and set her apart from everyone else. She could no longer count on Jeff's support. Instead, she'd have to rely on herself. She realized that no matter what the cost, she must remember.

* * * *

Susan ran down the path like a deer prancing through the woods. She was sure where each foot went and which protruding rocks became potential dangers. She knew every twist and turn in the path. She didn't have a care in the world. She felt exhilarated.

Momentarily, she paused to make sure Kelly and that other girl were following. In the near distance she could hear the crushing of leaves and twigs. They must be close behind, but they didn't seem to be in a hurry.

She decided to wait for them. This was, after all, the end of the journey. She had reached the edge of the precipice and Susan felt drawn to the drop off. She wondered what it would feel like to fall.

"Well?" Kelly's voice interrupted Susan's thoughts.

Susan turned. Kelly was standing with her hands on her hips, her legs spread apart. The other girl stood several feet back to her left. "What?" she asked.

"Where is it?" Kelly repeated.

Susan turned back to the precipice, its hidden but real dangers once again hypnotized her. Her eyes followed the fallen tree which connected the two cliffs, serving as a bridge.

A bridge to death.

"Over there," Susan said. "On the other side."

She couldn't help but smile. "You can almost see it from here."

"How do we get across?"

Susan detected a note of nervousness in Kelly's voice. She pointed to the fallen pine tree. "We use that as a bridge."

"You're crazy," Kelly said. There was a vacant stare on her face.

"You don't have a choice, Kelly."

With a faint cry, Kelly recoiled.

"In a few seconds, I'm going to go across, if you don't want to come, then stay. But don't ever expect me to be your friend. And don't expect anyone else to be your friend either. Because I'll tell."

"I don't want to go," Kelly said. There was a wild look in her eyes, a mixture of terror and beseeching. "Please don't make me go," she pleaded.

"Last chance, Kelly dear." Susan rested her hands on her hips.

Kelly's face was streaked with tears. "Pllllease."

Susan stared at Kelly.

Kelly took a step forward and stopped, her mouth agape.

Susan frowned.

Kelly took another step forward.

And another.

Susan smiled triumphantly. "Go on," she said as she motioned with her head.

Kelly's skin was pale as she tried to balance herself on the log. With one foot still resting on the ground, and the other on the log, she looked up at Susan, her eyes pleading.

Susan's expression did not change. Instead, she continued to stare at Kelly.

Kelly's hands formed into tight fists and her body went rigid. She breathed rapidly. She began to walk across the log, very carefully and slowly putting one foot in front of the other. She did this until she was about one-third of the way through.

"Go on," Susan urged. She felt like a hunter would when he's about to pull the trigger on his first quarry.

"I can't," she mumbled. Fear forced her to become immobile.

"Go!"

A small animal-like sound escaped from Kelly's mouth. She took another step and lost her balance. She tried to correct it by leaning to her right but that only caused her to totter some more.

Susan held her breath, her heart thumping wildly with excitement.

For a long time, Kelly stood there and Susan quickly grew bored. It was no fun just watching her stand there. Susan wanted to see her totter. She wanted to taste Kelly's fear. A few rocks should work wonders. Susan bent down and picked up two rocks about the size of large marbles.

By the time Susan returned her gaze to Kelly she was again walking, this time with confidence. She was halfway through and it seemed as if she were going to finish with no additional problems.

Susan looked down at her hands. She was still clutching the rocks. She threw one of them at Kelly's feet. Kelly lost her balance and tottered again.

Susan screeched with delight.

Susan threw the other.

It hit Kelly on the right leg, and she cried out in pain. But still the little bitch maintained her balance. Susan bent down to pick up some more, when someone jumped on top of her, forcing her down to the ground. It was Kelly's friend, the one who always followed them around.

"Get off me, you little bitch!" Susan threw handfuls of dirt and stones every direction she could. Susan formed a fist and as hard as she could, she swung her arm, aiming at her cheek. The impact sent Kelly's friend twirling down.

Susan looked back up at Kelly. She was heading back this way and had almost reached the end.

"Go back," Susan ordered.

Kelly refused and kept on coming.

Susan had, up to this point, been able to control her emotions. But as she saw Kelly coming toward her—disobeying her—she began to lose control. In vain Susan tried to suppress her anger—she breathed in deeply, she formed fists and released them, then formed them again.

With each step Kelly took, Susan could feel the pressure build up inside her like a volcano. With a scream that emerged from somewhere deep inside her, Susan stood up, rushed over to Kelly, her arms tautly in front of her.

"Go back!" Susan screeched and pushed her. Pushed her harder than she had intended to. For one long, violent second, Susan recognized the look of terror in Kelly's face. Her huge eyes and her burning skin made Susan think that for some reason Kelly couldn't breathe. But this wasn't the case, for in the next second Kelly opened her mouth and let out a blood curdling scream.

A scream that continued to ring in Susan's ears long after Kelly had fallen, long after she had landed with a dull thud.

Susan forced herself to look down over the precipice. Kelly was lying, face up, very still. Her eyes remained opened staring forever at nothing.

Susan threw her head back and laughed.

And laughed.

* * * *

Susan sat at the edge of the bed, trying to understand what she had just remembered. An involuntary tremor rippled deep within her, and she shook herself, hoping to dislodge the creeping discomfort.

My God! Did I really kill Kelly? No, of course not. It was just an unfortunate accident.

But I pushed her!

Susan felt the four walls closing in. Tighter and tighter. She wanted to run away from the memories, but worse, from the realization. If she had been capable of murder, then what of Timmy? Did she, in a fit of anger, slash out at him then block all memory of the heinous act? She had done precisely this with Kelly's death.

Susan looked down at her trembling hands.

She saw blood. They were covered with blood.

I stood at the top of the cliff staring down at Kelly's inert body. I never touched her blood. Never. NEVER!

Oh, dear God, then whose blood do I remember? Oh, Timmy, my son, where are you? What have I done? The scream that had been building inside of her erupted from deep within her.

Jeff came running into the bedroom, pale as snow. "What? Who?" His eyes darted from one place to the other.

"I did it!" Susan screamed.

Jeff grabbed her by her arms, his grip hard and forceful. "I can't understand you," he said.

"I did!" Susan yelled. "I did!"

He shook her. "Did what? What are you talking about?"

"Oh, help me. Please help me."

He shook her again.

Susan continued to scream.

He slapped her.

The sting of his palm on her cheek forced her to calm down. Large tears streamed down her face. Susan rubbed her cheek. "I killed her," she said.

Jeff immediately let her go, as if by touching her he would become contaminated. His eyes were opened wide and he stared at her as if she had suddenly transformed into a hideous monster. "Timmy?" he asked, taking one step back.

"Kelly," Susan answered, her mouth as dried as cracked dirt. "Kelly." Susan was having trouble breathing. "I killed Kelly. My God! I KILLED KELLY." She started to scream.

Her vision blurred. Objects were losing their shape.

First, the world turned gray, then black.

Chapter Twenty-Five

As soon as Susan opened her eyes, the memories came rushing back like hurricane winds. In those next few seconds, when she wasn't really quite awake but she wasn't still sleeping, she vainly hoped that it had all been a nightmare. With a sharp pain in the pit of her stomach, she realized it was a nightmare—a living nightmare!

"Mrs. Haynes?" A middle-aged man with a receding hair line and a big pot belly was squatting next to Susan. "Can you hear me?"

Who are you? Susan thought. She had never seen this man before. She nodded.

"You fainted," he said and as though he had read Susan's mind, he added, "I'm John Lopez, a paramedic. Your husband called us."

Susan looked past the man's shoulders. Jeff was standing in the background. His hands were shoved deep into his pants pockets and his head was hanging.

With the paramedic's help, Susan sat up.

"How do you feel?" he asked.

"Fine."

"What happened?"

"I fainted. I guess."

He looked up at the ceiling. "Why did you faint?"

"I...when I was...I remembered...something."

"I see," he said, although it was obvious he didn't. "I monitored your vital signs and everything seems normal, but I would suggest you pay a visit to your family physician, or if you prefer, we'll take you to the hospital."

"No. No hospital."

"If you refuse to go to the hospital, you'll have to sign a release form." He handed Susan a paper, and she immediately signed it even though she hadn't read it, something she had never done before. She shoved it back toward the paramedic.

"If you still feel dizzy, elevate your feet. That will keep the pressure in the upper extremities," he said.

"That won't be necessary," Susan answered and stood up to show him she was well.

"Then I guess you won't need us anymore," he said. He pointed to his partner, a youthful looking man with boyish-type good looks who strongly smelled of cologne.

Susan nodded and tempted a smile. "Thank you both," Susan looked at the second paramedic, "for coming," she said.

"Take care, Mrs. Haynes." They gathered their belongings, put them in their cases and carried them out. Jeff followed the men through the door.

* * * *

"What now?" Susan asked as soon as Jeff stepped back inside. He looked so sad, his unblinking eyes seemed huge and vacant. A deep sigh shook his body.

"I want you to know that I love you," he said.

But? Susan nodded.

"Good. Always remember—no matter what

happens—that I love you very much." The way he cleared his throat, Susan knew he was having trouble communicating. "Susan, what I have to say isn't easy for me." He wiped his face with the palm of his hand. "You see, right now I'm having trouble living with myself."

Susan opened her mouth to protest, but a wave of his hand dismissed that idea.

"I feel like a hypocrite," he continued rather quickly. "I come home every day like a good husband. I'm trying to believe in you and support you." Tears gathered in his eyes. "The truth is I really don't know if you hurt our son, and I can't live with you unless I know the truth." The tears ran down his cheek and he wiped them away angrily. "Please understand," he begged. "It's not you. It's me. I have to find the answer."

His words bored into Susan's soul. "Are you leaving me?" She held her head high, even though her insides were falling apart.

Unable to answer, he nodded and quickly looked down at the floor.

"Where will you go?" Susan fought hard to control the quiver in her voice.

"The club. A motel. A friend's house." His voice was drained of all emotion. He was quiet for a few seconds before continuing, "I really don't know, but it doesn't really matter." He headed toward the bedroom, and without turning around, he added, "Nothing matters anymore."

Susan sat on the couch while he packed. Later, she saw him walk out. He didn't say anything as he brushed past her on his way out.

Chapter Twenty-Six

Mary set her suitcase by the front door and flopped herself on the couch. Yesterday, she had left in such a hurry, her mind eaten away by worry, that she had forgotten to pack half of the things she needed. Not that she had any use for them. After all, she had returned within twenty-four hours, her mind at ease.

Knowing that things in Pine Basin were as they should be, she would now be able to devote her full attention to helping Susan find Timmy, and more importantly, she'd be able to call David and tell him to ease off. His threats to call the police would be useless.

She was about to pick up the phone when it began to ring. "Hello?"

"Mary." She recognized Jeff's voice and her heart caught in her throat.

"Timmy?" she asked.

"Still no word."

Mary sighed in relief. Jeff had sounded so pitiful she had assumed the worst. "What's wrong?"

"I...left Susan."

"Oh, Jeff."

"Mary, I couldn't stay any longer. Everything points to Susan. And I love Timmy so much." His voice sounded broken, like someone whose life had been drained from him. "And Susan too. But I just can't stay. Please go to her, but don't tell her I sent you."

* * * *

Shortly after Jeff left, Susan sat on the couch and felt the warmth of the afternoon evaporate, leaving only the coldness behind. The ringing of the doorbell brought her out of her trance-like existence. She looked up at the scenic picture clock above the fireplace. Timmy had always said that the painting made him want to go fishing. Susan sighed. It was only 7:18.

The doorbell rang again.

This time Susan got up to answer it.

"Mary," she said and opened the door wider, allowing her friend to enter.

Immediately, Mary threw her arms around Susan. Mary had promised Jeff not to let Susan know he had sent her, so she decided to tell a small white lie. "I saw Jeff leaving with his suitcases. I've been waiting for your call ever since then. I couldn't wait anymore. Do you need me?"

Unable to answer, Susan nodded.

"What happened?"

"He, uh, couldn't take the pressure of living with me. Not knowing one way or the other..." She shrugged.

"He'll be back, honey." She squeezed Susan tighter. "After he's had time to think, he'll realize that you could never harm anyone. It's not in your nature. He'll be back."

"I doubt it," Susan answered. "He's lost all his faith in me. If that's gone, everything else is also gone." Susan felt the same void that had first grasped her when she realized that Timmy had disappeared.

"He does love you," Mary said.

Susan shrugged. "It doesn't matter." She flopped herself down on the couch. "I've been so caught up with my own problems, I haven't even asked how you're doing. I tried calling you several times, but you weren't home."

Mary wet her lips. "I figured you had. I tried to call and let you know I was leaving town, but I couldn't reach you."

"You left town? Where did you go?"

"It's my mom again. She had another heart attack. But she's doing okay."

A stab of guilt spread through Susan's insides as she remembered thinking that Mary was avoiding her. "Mary, I'm sorry. If there's anything I can do."

"No, there's nothing anybody can do, including me. Anyway I came home because I wanted to be with you. I've hired a nurse to take care of Mother. She'll be fine."

"Can you afford to do that?"

"She's got insurance." She attempted a weak smile. "Don't worry. She's fine, really. She's being a terrible grouch and I'd really rather be here with you. I know you didn't ask my advice, but do you want me to tell you what I think you should do?"

"What?"

"Get yourself together. Look at you! You look like a mess. I want you to go put some make-up, comb your hair."

"Mary, I don't feel like—"

"And you're calling up your principal. Tell him you'll be back to work on Monday."

"The sub has already been lined up. That person is counting on working on Monday."

"Tuesday, then."

"I—"

"Call!"

Susan opened her mouth to protest, but she knew Mary was right. Susan sighed and nodded. She reached for the address book, looked up her principal's number and dialed. When she heard him answer the phone, her voice caught in her throat.

"Hello!" he repeated.

"Mr. Hensley? It's me Susan. Susan Haynes."

Now it was his turn to freeze. When he did speak, his tone seemed unnaturally sweet. "Susan, it's good to hear from you. What's the news?"

"None, yet, and it's killing me just to sit around and wait. I'd like to go back to work. Monday, if possible. If not, Tuesday."

There was silence on the other end. Then, "Susan, uh, that's not such a good idea. Our superintendent feels...that is, the parents... I really believe that with all of your problems, you don't need to add teaching responsibilities. Relax. Stay home and—"

"Mr. Hensley, has my position been filled?"

The answer came much too quickly. "No. No. Of course not. Mrs. Gunther is just a sub."

"Then why can't you release her?"

"Well, of course, I can release her any time. It's just that...that..."

"Has the superintendent talked to you about me?"

"Well, as a matter of fact, yes."

"What did he say?"

"He feels that, uh, the—what can I say?—the negative publicity surrounding you would not be so good for our school."

"Does this mean I've been fired?"

"Oh, no. Goodness, no. You're just on a leave-of-absence. Like I said, Mrs. Gunther is only a sub." Seeing that Susan didn't answer, he continued, "Susan, believe me. I'm sorry."

"Me too, Mr. Hensley. I'll get in touch with you

later." Susan kept the receiver by her ear long after he had hung up, hoping he'd change his mind.

Mary's squeezed Susan's shoulder. "I'm sorry, Susan," she said softly.

Susan shrugged. "I should have expected it. Everyone thinks I'm guilty. Sometimes I think I'm guilty."

"Most of the time, do you feel that way?"

Susan shook her head.

"Deep down, do you feel you hurt him in any way?"

Again Susan shook her head. This time more emphatically.

"That's how I feel too," Mary said.

She spoke with such confidence, such knowledge. Susan wished she too could be that confident. "How can you be so sure, Mary?"

"Because I know you."

An image of Kelly sprawled at the bottom of the cliff, her face forever frozen in fear invaded Susan's mind. "Maybe you just think you know me. My past—"

"You did nothing wrong in your past."

"Oh, yes, I did."

Mary looked at Susan with a mixture of fear and curiosity. "Meaning?" She held her breath in anticipation.

"I...can't seem to remember anything other than that path."

Mary visibly breathed easier. "It's best to leave your past alone. Right now you have a responsibility to Timmy. Now promise me you'll drop this silly notion of yours to pursue your past—at least until Timmy is home."

Susan thought of Kelly and guilty feelings surfaced. Kelly, forgive me, she thought. I'll turn myself in later. I promise. But first I must find my son. Slowly, Susan nodded.

Chapter Twenty-Seven

The aroma of the cake still baking in the oven enticed Susan and drew her toward the kitchen. Later, when it was done, she saw that it was a huge birthday cake—more like a wedding cake—with seven perfectly round layers decorated with light yellow flowers. She tasted a bit of the icing and found it to be deliciously sweet.

She pulled a chair up to the table across from the cake, anticipating the moment she would cut out a piece of this enticing treat. As she reached out to touch it, the cake exploded, sending bits of icing throughout the room.

* * * *

Susan fought her way out of sleep like a drowning swimmer. She sat up, her body still shaking with the memory of the dream. She blinked and tried to catch her breath. The dream hadn't made any sense, but Susan had read somewhere that dreams were supposed to be symbolic. She searched her mind, trying to come up with some meaning. She glanced at Timmy's picture, and suddenly she knew.

It involved another cake, one in her childhood. Somehow it was important, but, unfortunately, she couldn't remember much else.

But at least she knew what the dream was trying to tell her. Timmy was alive, but only until his birthday. His birthday—oh God, that was tomorrow! She had to find him before then.

The ringing of the doorbell made her heart beat so much faster that she could hear its thrumming in her ears. Timmy, Timmy was all she could think of.

The doorbell rang again and Susan shot out of bed. She grabbed her robe and pulled it on as she ran toward the door.

"Who is it?" she asked from behind the closed door.

"It's me, Susan." She recognized Bronson's voice. "Open up."

Susan immediately unbolted the door and swung it open.

"No, Susan, no word on Timmy yet," he said, answering the question he knew Susan was probably going to ask. "I just want to talk. Do you have any coffee made?" He noticed Susan's uncombed hair and robe. "No, I suppose not. I got you out of bed, huh?"

"It's all right," Susan answered. "I should have been up a long time ago."

"You sure now?"

She nodded.

"Good," he said. "Then let's go make some coffee so we can talk." He let himself in and headed straight for the kitchen.

* * * *

"I heard you had some excitement here yesterday," Bronson said as he poured two heaping teaspoons of sugar into his coffee.

Susan placed the sugar bowl back on the counter, hoping that Bronson would say something else. But he was an expert at the game of saying little and refused to reveal any additional information. "You mean about Jeff," Susan said.

His eyebrows rose in an arch. "Jeff?"

"He left me."

"Aha." He stirred his coffee. "You must admit that he's under a lot of pressure. When he walked out, is that when you fainted?"

So that's what he was getting at. "No, I fainted before he left."

"Well, that was convenient for you."

Susan stared at him. Sometimes this man could be so exasperating.

He took a sip of coffee. "Excellent coffee. Have I ever told you that before?"

Susan nodded.

He tapped his head. "Of course I had. Where's my mind nowadays?" He took another sip. "So you fainted because..." His voice trailed off.

"I felt dizzy," she lied. "Too much worrying, I suppose."

"Aha. I thought maybe it had something to do with your past."

"No." Susan's rough voice gave her away.

"You know, Susan, my mama always used to tell me, 'The truth can set you free.'"

"What's that suppose to mean?"

"You need to find your past."

"I plan to." Susan felt uncomfortable. "Some day." An awkward silence followed. Every noise was magnified several times.

"The real reason I'm here—other than to sample your delicious coffee—is because I want you to be the first to know. We have Julie Ward under custody. We'll probably book her on kidnapping charges." He pushed his cup away.

Susan felt her heart skip a beat, then it picked up the pace. "I thought you had cleared her."

"No one is clear until we find Timmy."

"What about that lie detector test? I thought that showed her innocence," Susan played with the rim of her coffee cup.

"The machine is not foolproof," Bronson said. "If a person knows how to control his breathing rate and heart beat, he could conceivably lie and the machine wouldn't pick it up."

"Does she have my Timmy?"

Bronson sighed. "I wish to God I knew. But if she does, I don't know where. We've had her under surveillance for a while, and so far she hasn't led us to Timmy."

"Then why did you arrest her?"

"Because the girls at the daycare take turns going out to eat."

The surprised look on Susan's face made him chuckle. "I don't think I follow you," Susan said.

"No, of course, you don't. Let me explain. Mondays are Miss Ward's days to go out to eat. Ever since she began working there," he scratched his forehead, "oh, let me see, about three years ago now, she's been stopping at Joe's Café. Last Monday was the first day she's missed going to Joe's Café."

"Where did she go?" Susan held her breath.

"She says that for some reason she just wasn't hungry and went for a walk instead. She didn't meet or see anyone she knows, and no one saw her."

Susan felt Bronson was holding something back. "Why don't you believe her?"

"Because, Susan," he looked directly at her, his eyes narrow slits in his face, "we have a witness who swears she saw Miss Ward dragging a child behind her."

"And the child?" Susan asked, afraid to hear the answer.

"Fits the description of your son."

* * * *

Susan sat down.

Stood up.

Paced the floor.

Sat back down.

Changed positions.

She stood back up again, walked toward the wall, balled her hands into fists and banged them against the wall over and over. "Damn you, Julie Ward! What have you done with my boy?" She continued to slam her fists against the wall until her knuckles began to bleed. She dropped to the floor, her outstretched palms dragging down the wall. "Where are you, Timmy?"

She held her hands out in front of her and looked at them. They were red, but not as red as when they were covered with blood.

An uncontrollable chill swept her body as one question after another plowed through her mind like bullets out of a machine gun.

She had killed Kelly.

She pushed her. Kelly fell.

I stood there and—and God, help me—I laughed.

I never touched Kelly. I never touched her blood.

Then why, God, do I remember my hands covered with blood?

* * * *

Throughout the remainder of the day, Susan's vivid dream nibbled at her insides. I must reach

Timmy before his birthday. I must reach Timmy before his birthday. I must.

She heard Bronson's warning. "Stay by the phone. Make sure someone is always available to answer it." Jeff was gone. She had to stay by the phone.

Julie Ward could lead them to Timmy, and it was Susan's duty to be there for that possibility. But each second that dragged took her away from Pine Basin. Away from the truth. Away from Timmy.

If only she could complete the pieces to the puzzle which formed her past. She forced herself to concentrate on that elusive trail...

....and three girls. Kelly. Susan. And—and? Who was this third member of their group? Why was she always no more than a shadow?

Focus on that elusive figure. Will yourself to see her. Make it happen, Susan ordered herself. Like a fog slowly rising, the shape began to take form. She saw a little girl with a brown ponytail running, needing comfort. She was—

A sudden pounding in Susan's head disrupted her thoughts. Susan forced the pain aside.She was Daddy's girl, because Daddy knew the truth. But he wouldn't tell. He—

The beating inside Susan's head forced her to close her eyes to keep from falling.

He wouldn't tell anyone because he was...afraid—

Susan reached out and cradled her head in her hands. The pain forced her to her knees and in the flash of a second, when she closed her eyes to keep the world from spinning, she saw a sawed-off gun. It exploded, filling the room with blood.

Chapter Twenty-Eight

Susan's instincts told her to go to Pine Basin where Timmy was waiting for her. However, logic told her to stay and wait until she heard from Bronson. Susan decided to follow her instincts.

She picked up the phone to dial Mary's number, then slammed it down. Mary would be hurt if Susan didn't call her, but if she did call and told her about her plans, Mary might get mad. She was very much against Susan confronting her past. She knew Mary feared what might happen to Susan if she remembered too fast, too suddenly, but that was a chance Susan would have to take.

She again picked up the phone, but this time she dialed Bronson's number. "I'm sorry, but he's not in right now, Mrs. Haynes," said the male voice over the phone. "Do you want me to tell him to call you?"

"Please."

Susan hung up. Now all that was left was to notify Jeff. As she grabbed her car keys, new fears invaded Susan's mind. She was actually going to see Jeff.

* * * *

Susan was pleasantly surprised to see Jeff's

name on a door and, underneath his name, the words "VICE-PRESIDENT." He had made it after all. This realization stirred a string of emotions: happiness, depression, anger, and bitterness, all interwoven with love and forgiveness.

"Susan."

She turned.

Looking thinner and withdrawn, Jeff nevertheless seemed as dashing as ever in his navy blue suit. Susan noticed that he was still wearing the same tie Timmy had given him for Christmas. "Jeff," she said.

With all the awkwardness of a teenager on his first date, Jeff briefly hugged Susan. Then they stood staring at each other as though their thoughts were written on their faces.

"Let's go to my new office," he said.

"Congratulations."

He shrugged. "I really thought I'd be on cloud nine when I got this far. But I'm not." He pointed to a chair. "Sit down. Can I get you anything to drink?"

Susan shook her head.

"It's good to see you."

"I'm leaving, Jeff."

Pain crossed his eyes, and Susan wanted to reach out, but she refrained herself by grabbing the chair's arm rest. When he spoke, his voice was barely audible. "Are you here to ask me for a divorce?" His features were sunken, his eyes, lifeless.

Susan almost smiled. "No. I'm just here to tell you that I'm going back to New Mexico. You see, I've got this feeling deep inside of me that tells me that I'm finally able to confront my past. But most important, this knowledge will lead me to Timmy."

"Susan, you don't know that for sure." He

frowned, as though realizing that no matter what he said, she wasn't going to change her mind. "Does Dr. Orr know you're going to New Mexico?"

Susan shook her head.

Jeff sat on top of his desk, facing Susan. He reached for her hand and held it in both of his. "I don't like it. If you remember too much too fast, you could become catatonic. Dr. Orr has warned us of this over and over again. I'm sorry, Susan. It's just too dangerous. I won't let you go."

Susan jerked her hand away from his and stood up. "You have no choice. You gave up that privilege when you walked out on me. Good-bye, Jeff." Without turning back to look at him, she walked out, leaving behind a hollow spot in her heart.

* * * *

Susan's flight was due to depart in a little over an hour, and she still hadn't heard from Bronson. She was considering calling him when her doorbell rang.

Cold fingers of panic caught at her throat as she dashed to answer it. Please be all right, Timmy. Please be all right.

Susan swung the door open and stared at Bronson. He looked tired and somewhat older. Perhaps it was an illusion caused by the dark smudges under his eyes. His shoulders sagged, and his head hung low. His frightening appearance tested Susan's endurance. She stood rigidly, trembling, sweat beginning to run down her back and on her forehead.

Bronson's eyebrows arched in surprise. "Susan, no, I'm sorry. It's nothing like that. Still no word on Timmy."

A small animal-like sound escaped from her mouth. "Thank God," she said as she opened the door wider, letting him in. "It's just that every time I see you, I think that...and you look so..." She stopped and shook her head. "Can I get you anything to drink?" This time he didn't make himself at home, but stood in the entry way, his weight shifting from one foot to the other. Susan led him to the den where they sat down. "Coffee?"

"No. No thanks. I have to get home. Poor Carol—that's my wife—I think she's ready to divorce me. She never sees me." He smirked. "I promised her I'd get home early today."

"I'm sorry," Susan said.

"Yeah, well, I guess that's what I get for being the tough detective everyone expects miracles from." He shrugged. "We released Miss Ward."

Damn! Susan closed her eyes.

"Seems our witness wasn't quite reliable. A couple of hours ago, she told us how she saw Miss Ward dragging this light-brown headed kid. And the kid was just screaming and yelling. She saw it all in her crystal ball!" He raked his hair with his fingers. "Her crystal ball! And there's more. She also knows who's been doin' all those convenience store robberies. She sees him everyday in her crystal ball!"

As he spoke, Susan sat very quietly on the edge of the couch, her clasped hands resting on her lap.

"Hey, I'm sorry," he said. "I'm dumpin' all of these problems in your lap as though you didn't have enough of your own."

Susan stood up and walked toward the window and stared out. It was a cloudy evening filled with grayness. "You're not dumping problems on me. He's my son, remember? I want to know what's going on."

"Really?"

Susan turned and stared at him. He sat and held her eyes. She nodded, looked away, and continued to look out of the window. Instinctively, she knew she wasn't going to like what he had to say.

"I'm getting a lot of hassle from the D.A.," he began. "First he says that I'm spending too much time on this case. Then he says that he wants it closed and closed now. But since we have no Timmy we can't really close it." Susan turned to look at him. He wet his lips, cleared his throat, and continued, "He feels that the case would be closed if we arrested you."

Susan stared not at Bronson, but at the wall as though she expected it to move any minute. "What proof do you have?"

"We have a television tape where you admit seeing your hands covered with blood."

"But that wasn't Timmy's blood," she protested.

"You know it and I know it. But we can't prove it. All we have is your testimony and your background to go on," Bronson said.

"That's not fair!" Susan shouted. "I haven't been back to see Dr. Orr, so no one could say I'm seeing a shrink."

"The point is you were seeing him at the time of Timmy's disappearance."

"Is that a crime?"

"No, of course not." His tone was softer, his looks convincing.

"Are you here to arrest me?"

Slowly, he shook his head. "No, but the next time I come, it'll be for one of two reasons: to hand Timmy over to you or to arrest you." He stood up.

"Before you go," Susan said and Bronson sat back down, "if you pardon the cliché, am I free to leave town?"

"It would look mighty suspicious if you did."

He leaned back. "Where were you planning to go?"

"Oh, nowhere. I'm not leaving. I was just asking to see how serious you were about arresting me."

"Aha. I see." He stood up again. "Hang around town so I can contact you and of course I can reach Jeff at work or at his apartment. Right?"

Susan nodded.

"Great, but of course I won't have to because I'll be able to reach you here. Right?"

Again, Susan nodded.

"Good. In that case, I must go home before I end up without a wife."

He stopped by the door, "About the new developments, Susan, I'm sorry, but you have my word that if need be, on my own time, I will continue to look for Timmy.

Chapter Twenty-Nine

Mary didn't like it one bit. She had called Susan several times, and Susan hadn't answered the phone. Wasn't she suppose to hang around the house in case of an emergency? Unless, of course, they had already found Timmy. But no, that wasn't very likely. Susan would have called.

The one thing Mary was certain about was that Susan wasn't home. Maybe she was out with Jeff. They could have gone out to eat. Heck, they might even spend the night together. Possible, but not likely.

Knowing Susan like she did, Mary knew Susan wouldn't go out with Jeff, leaving the phone unattended. She'd be at home, waiting for the phone to ring.

So why wasn't she home? Could it be that Susan felt that maybe she was more useful somewhere else? Some place like Pine Basin?

Was it possible that Susan had—in spite of her promise not to—returned to Pine Basin? If so, what if she remembered everything? In a few minutes Susan could destroy what Mary had spent more than half of her life trying to build. Mary could not allow this to happen.

She'd wait one more hour, maybe two. Then, if

Susan still wasn't home, she would hire a private plane to fly her into Pine Basin. Chances were that Susan had taken a commercial plane, in which case, it would have landed in El Paso. There, she would have to rent a car, then drive the two and a half hours to Pine Basin. With luck Susan might even spend the night in El Paso, then drive up the next morning. If so, then Mary would still arrive in Pine Basin in time to stop Susan from doing any real harm.

* * * *

Located in the heart of Lincoln National Forest, Pine Basin was a typical summer and winter playground for the wealthy. Its main street was lined with motels, cabins, real-estate offices, restaurants, and curio shops which buzzed with the excitement of noisy shoppers, their sacks rustling against each other as they made their way from one store to the other. Normally, they welcomed the cool mountain breeze, unlike the hot, gusty desert winds which surrounded the national forest.

Susan, oblivious to the shoppers and to the aroma of freshly smoked brisket for which Pine Basin was famous, drove past the curio shops, past the newly renovated McFields High School, past the new Presbyterian church, and out toward the edge of town. She had no idea why, other than it "felt right."

There, she found a worn-out motel called the Happy Days Inn. One end of the motel's sign hung lower than the other, being held up with a twist of baling wire. It squealed like a pig even in the slightest of winds. Susan stared at the dilapidated motel skeptically, then back toward the newer looking motels less than two blocks away. She shrugged and pulled into the Happy Days Inn's vacant parking lot.

As Susan walked into the office, an old man with a yellow, wrinkled, gummy complexion dropped the paper he was reading and stared at her through rheumy eyes.

"I need a room," she said.

He continued to stare.

"Do you have one?" Susan asked.

"Yeah, I got plenty of rooms. What do you need?"

"I'm by myself. One with a single bed will be fine."

He nodded and handed Susan a registration form to fill out. She signed it Sue Haynes.

"That'll be thirty-four dollars 'n thirty-six cents," he said.

Susan handed him two twenties, and as he gave her the change he asked, "Are you planning to be here long?" He looked down at the registration form. "Miss, uh..." he deliberately stared at Susan, smiling with yellow, tobacco stained teeth, "Miss Haynes, Sue Haynes," he said as though he knew better.

"I'm not sure how long I'll be here," Susan said.

He handed her the key. "You're in "Room Ten. That's across the office and to your left," he said. Susan thanked him and walked out. She could feel his eyes following her.

As she opened the rented blue Chevy's trunk to retrieve her suitcase, a small airplane soared above her. Susan glanced up and wondered what it was possibly doing here. It seemed to be so much out of place in this peaceful community.

* * * *

"Here you are," said the pilot. He opened the small plane's door and let Mary out. "First time

I've been here. How about you?"

"I've been here several times before."

"Then I suppose you know where to go, huh?"

"Oh, yes," said Mary, grabbing her small suitcase. "I know exactly where I need to go."

Chapter Thirty

Now that she was here, Susan knew she had made the right decision, but the task before her lay like a giant puzzle. Where should she begin? Almost immediately the answer came to her: she could use the telephone book to do some basic research.

She knew that her maiden name was McFields. If there were any McFields listed in the telephone book, chances were that they were her relatives.

She glanced at the night stand which was in desperate need of a new coat of paint. The motel was too old to have a modern convenience like a telephone in each room, but Susan had noticed that there was a public phone booth across the street. Quickly, she grabbed her purse, the room key, and left.

Susan carefully studied the telephone book as though it was a Bible. There were no McFields, and after searching for any Maynards, Susan found out that the operator had been right: there were no Maynards either. Now what? Disgustedly, Susan slammed the directory shut and stared at it.

Maybe the yellow pages would give her some ideas or revive some tucked-away memory. She found a McFields Hardware Store, a McFields Park, and even a McFields Feed Store, which, according to the small ad, provided feed to most of the areas' ranches—including Pine Basin Ranch.

A tiny spark, like a flashlight whose batteries are mostly worn out, passed through Susan's brain. Pine Basin Ranch...

Of course! That was the name of her childhood home, but there was more. That was also the place where— Where what? Susan bit her lip as she forced herself to think. Yes, that was it! This is where the Secret Place is! The woods which surrounded her childhood mansion also housed the Secret Place.

This was where she'd begin.

* * * *

As Susan drove to the Secret Place, she watched with concern the gathering of the threatening clouds. They drifted in with a sudden fury, changing the sky from a soft blue to a gray and finally to a gray-black. It covered the forest in darkness, leaving a feeling of heaviness hanging in the air. It was as if night was lurking behind the trees, waiting to spring on Susan. Time had become a creeping enemy.

But in spite of the ominous shadows, Susan continued to drive down the bumpy, winding, dirt road. She knew this road also led her to her childhood house, but she fought the urge to go there. She had to find the Secret Place. She was in the general vicinity. She could feel it. But, she wondered, would she be able to recognize it after all these years?

Abruptly, she brought the car to a halt and stared at an ancient ponderosa pine. Its furthest limb had long since died, but it still hung on to the tree with solemn determination. It pointed to the gloomy foot trail which would lead to the Secret Place.

Apprehension settled around Susan, her eyes glued to the gloomy path. She stepped out of the car and made her way toward the pine tree. The dark, threatening forest surrounded her.

To a newcomer, the trail would have been hardly recognizable as such. But Susan shouldn't have worried. She was familiar with each curve and turn it offered even though it had changed with time. New growth had eliminated parts of the path, creating new twists and turns, but basically it was still the same, as ancient as earth itself.

Above her, the massive clouds further drowned the forest in deep shadows. Somewhere in front of her, thunder erupted as lightning cracked into life. The storm turned the day gray, the color of hopelessness.

Susan swallowed hard and continued to walk deep into the forest, deep into her past.

* * * *

"Please don't walk so fast," Kelly begged.
But Susan only went faster.
"Don't leave me," she begged. "Don't leave me."

* * * *

Susan stopped to catch her breath. She had obviously been running, but for how long, she couldn't tell. Perspiration collected on the upper part of her lip. How much further, she wondered. A deep rumble of thunder vibrated throughout the forest, and she shuddered as a sudden gust of cold wind caressed her body. "Timmy!" she screamed.

Feeling desperate, she broke into a run, like a

deer running from a hunter. She scraped her arm against a tree, the burning sensation sending an electric wave of pain through her nerve center. "Timmy!" she screamed again. Feeling a tightness in her throat, she tried to swallow. The forest beckoned her just as it had so many years ago. A prickling at the back of Susan's neck warned her that something wasn't quite right.

* * * *

"I'm afraid," Kelly said.

"Me too," Susan answered. "Let's go back."

"I can't." Kelly seemed on the verge of tears. "She'll tell everyone. I won't have any friends."

"I'll be your friend," Susan said, reaching for her hand.

"That's not enough," Kelly said, yanking her hand away.

* * * *

Susan stared at her hands. She and Kelly had walked down together, fearing the forest, as though it had become an entity in its own right. How could that be? She remembered running ahead of Kelly and the other girl.

As Susan stood staring out into the ominous forest, tentacles of fear stretched out and strangled her. Then, her eyes focused on the decaying pine which had fallen, serving as a bridge between the two cliffs. She dragged herself toward the edge. Without looking down, she knew the cliff before her dropped some forty or fifty feet. She had arrived.

As she stood spellbound, a bolt of lightning flashed through the forest. Its loud, growl of thunder seemed like a gruff voice, laughing at her terror. The savage gray sky became twice as threatening.

Involuntarily she looked down over the precipice. A tiny body lay in its shadow.

"Timmy!" she screamed at the top of her lungs.

Chapter Thirty-One

The closer Mary got to the Pine Basin Ranch cut-off, the more convinced she became that she had made a drastic mistake. She should have called Marilyn, let her know she was coming. As it was, there already existed a cloud of doubt and mistrust between them.

Mary spotted a telephone booth in front of the Pic Pac convenience store. Letting out a long sigh, Mary yielded to her inner voice. She pulled into the parking lot.

As she stepped out of the car, she heard someone call her. It was the store manager who had just finished with his shift. "Hey, Mrs. Logan," he said. "I thought you had already gone back to Dallas."

"I had to come back. I...uh...left some things behind that I needed," Mary lied.

"Yeah? Well, I bet your daughter is happy you forgot 'em. She was just here a little while ago."

"Marilyn? Marilyn was here?" Something gnawed at her. Something like a forbidden thought, but before it could blossom, she quickly pushed it back to the recess of her mind.

"Yeah," he answered completely unaware of Mary's growing panic. "She came to pick up some toys—you know, like a gun and those little cars—and some candy."

Mary felt her heart catch in her throat. It couldn't be happening again. She jumped back into the car and sped off, throwing a hurried "thanks" over her shoulder.

* * * *

Susan leaned back against the piñon pine. Her breath came in sharp, short gasps, her mind refusing to accept what her eyes had seen. In a gesture of self-defense, she had shut her eyes tightly; and now, as she reopened them, they focused not on Timmy's body, but on a four foot piece of wood. Her eyes watered when she realized that it wasn't Timmy down there. Instead, it was only a portion of a decaying tree trunk. Her mind had played a horrible trick on her. True, the precipice's hungry bottom had once held a body in its greedy jaws, but that had been a long time ago.

In certain areas, part of the wood had rotted and small bits and pieces lay like dust in the indented trunk. But years of decaying had not deteriorated it enough to render it useless. As Susan contemplated the log, it was so easy to picture Kelly trying to balance herself on it. She was like an old woman who had had a few too many martinis and could no longer steady her shaking hands.

* * * *

Susan's mouth slackened in hopeless anguish as she watched Kelly try to balance on the wood. Please be careful, Kelly, Susan thought. Don't fall. Oh, please, don't—

Kelly, desperate to reach safety, abruptly

looked up to see how much further she still had to walk. In so doing, she lost her balance. A subdued, hysterical sound escaped from Susan's throat. She wanted to help her friend, but fear paralyzed her and weighed down her mind. Susan was able to breathe easier only when Kelly regained her equilibrium. The experience had made Kelly more careful so that now she slowly dragged her feet along the stump.

Good, good girl, Susan thought, or maybe she said it aloud. She couldn't remember. One thing for sure, she wasn't going to scream and show Kelly her fear.

* * * *

Susan stood shivering, feeling the wind blow through her hair, just as it had that fateful day so many years ago. The memory, the images—they had now vanished and Susan closed her eyes trying to bring them back. Immediately, a pain surged through her head, dulling her senses and draining all of her energy and hope. Susan cradled her head in her hands.

NO!

She would not let those cursed headaches take over, even though the pain in her head made all of the objects in the forest seem double-imaged. She leaned against a tree for support while she rubbed her eyes, attempting to re-adjust her vision. With each pounding sensation, her hopes of remembering faded like a light in a fog. For the first time since this nightmare began, Susan began to think that maybe Mary was right: Timmy's disappearance could not possibly be linked with Kelly's death.

Susan felt like a fool. The thought that she

might never see Timmy again tore at her heart. Oh, son where are you?

I want to help you, but I don't know how. I was sure that once I got here all the missing pieces of this horrible jigsaw puzzle would fall right in place. I was so certain that I can almost hear your bright, cheery laughter peeling like happy bells. The memory of Timmy's soft little giggle almost made Susan want to smile.

But you're not really laughing, are you, son? Your little arms are reaching out for help; your face—your lovable, tiny face—is pleading for mercy.

And I can't help you.

Oh, God!

A sob shook Susan's body and that—or maybe the pain volleying back and forth in her head—forced her to her knees. She wept large tears, shaking the soul out of her body.

I can't help you, my son. Can't...

Mommyyy.

Wide-eyed, Susan stared all around her. Then a sharp pain hit Susan in the pit of her stomach when she realized that Timmy's voice—so clear to her—was only in her mind. Susan could see his mischievous eyes and smiling mouth. His arms, reaching, grasping. "I want to hug you, Mommy."

I want to hug you, too.

And I'm sorry. So sorry.

Sorry that I can't help.

Sorry.

Slowly, as though moving in slow motion, Susan looked up.

I can stop her, Susan thought. I'm not afraid.

Not anymore.

* * * *

"Turn back, Kelly!" Susan screeched as Kelly tottered on the log.

"You can do it, Kelly," Susan coached. She forced her voice to sound as calm and soothing as possible. "Take a deep breath. Don't look down, slowly turn around, and begin to walk toward me."

Kelly stood frozen, fear paralyzing her.

"It's okay, Kelly. Take your time." Silently, Susan slowly counted. One, two, three, four, five. "Okay, Kelly. Now you can do it. Turn around slowly."

Susan held her breath as she watched her. It was working. Kelly seemed to be gaining confidence. "Good!" Susan said as her hopes soared. "You're doing great," she encouraged as she watched Kelly slowly turn around. "Now walk toward me. Slowly."

Kelly did and Susan smiled triumphantly.

Kelly was safe. She was going to make it after all.

But just as Kelly was ready to claim that victory, she lost her concentration. Rocks were flying past her; some even hit her legs.

She looked up, first startled; then realizing their source, panic covered her face like a blanket. The more she stared, the more she seemed to sway back and forth. Large tears streamed down her cheeks as she tried to dodge the flying stones.

For a while—it seemed forever—Susan sat there, staring. Unmoving. This can't be happening, she thought. With mechanical movements, she moved toward the source. Susan tried to stop them, but was too weak and too late. She reached out as though she could really grab Kelly and rescue her.

But as Susan reached out, Kelly tumbled. Susan knew that this time, it was over. Kelly wasn't going to regain her balance. Not now. Not ever.

"No!" Susan bellowed, dragging herself to the edge. Kelly lay at the bottom, very still. Her tiny body had landed in a unnatural "S" position.

Susan scurried down the cliff. "Please be okay," she said. She almost fell, but held onto a branch. "Please be okay," she repeated. Large tears blurred her vision.

In her hurry, Susan scraped her elbow. The pain shot up her arm, but she ignored it.

"Kelly!" she shouted.

There was no answer.

Susan stood by her, afraid to touch her. Afraid not to touch her. Her tiny body had never seemed so fragile before. Susan knelt down beside her. With a trembling hand, Susan touched her shoulder. "K-Kelly?" Susan barely mouthed the word.

Kelly did not answer.

Susan scooped her up in her arms and cradled her. "Oh, Kelly. Kelly. Kelly." For a long time, it seemed forever, she stayed there, cradling her friend, the tears running down her cheeks onto Kelly's face, as though she too mourned her untimely death.

Susan wanted to cry and scream. Get back at the world—at fate—for taking her friend. Gently, as though afraid to hurt Kelly if she moved her suddenly, she laid her back down. Susan's hands, arms, and dress were covered with blood.

Kelly's blood.

Susan stared at them in wild horror. She plastered her hands to her face and screamed.

The sound of laughter forced her to stop screaming.

Susan looked up...and up—toward the direction of the laughter.

The girl stood at the edge of the cliff, her head thrown back, the wind blowing her blond hair in all directions. She was laughing. But who was she?

Susan closed her eyes in an effort to concentrate. Logically, this blond girl standing at the edge of the cliff, laughing, must had been the third member of the group—the obscure shadow Susan had never been able to focus on.

But that was wrong.

The laughing girl on the cliff was blond.

Susan had always been a brunette.

The girl who tried to save Kelly had been a brunette—just like her. Tears flooded Susan's eyes as she realized that she hadn't killed Kelly after all.

For some reason the memories Susan had been remembering were not her own but those of...who?

Susan forced herself to concentrate in spite of the screaming pain inside her head. Who was this mysterious shadow? A name flashed before her, but before she could grasp it, it was gone.

Concentrate!

It was...it was...Marilyn!

Marilyn—Mary's daughter.

Susan broke into a run, a cloud of anxiety hovering over her. She no longer ran like a deer. Instead, she was a child escaping a nightmare.

Her eyes tried to focus on the obstacles in the path, but she often found that she couldn't avoid the rotting, fallen trunks. She stumbled several times, but each time she pushed on harder, making up for lost time.Although both of her heels were bruised and tender, she didn't care. Her mind had become a one-track mind: she must find Timmy.

And Marilyn would lead her to him.

If only it wasn't too late.

Chapter Thirty-Two

Nestled in a stand of ponderosa pine on the southeastern corner of Pine Basin Ranch stood a seventy-five to eighty-five foot long mansion. Its tall, marble columns gave it the appearance of a Southern plantation. Even though it spoke of elegance, all Mary could see was the cloud of tension which enveloped Susan's childhood residence. From the safety of her car, Mary tried to stare through its many windows, hoping to catch a hint of movement inside the house.

Mary remained perfectly still, as watchful as a bird ready for flight. But no matter how much she stared at the windows, she couldn't detect any sign of life inside the mansion.

Mary sighed as she stepped out of the car. Her feet dragged along the tiled walkway as she forced herself to walk toward the front door. She reached into her purse and fished out the house keys. For a fraction of a second, she considered turning back. Then she rubbed her eyes, took a deep breath, and opened the door. She stepped into the foyer and saw Marilyn leaning against the archway leading into the living room. Marilyn held her hands behind her.

"Hello, Mama," she said. "What are you doing here?"

"You have him, don't you?"

"Is that a question or an accusation?"

"Damn it, Marilyn. Answer me! Do you have Timmy?" Mary felt the blood pounding in her veins. She curled her fingers into fists in an effort to control herself. Then alarm replaced anger as she watched her daughter's eyes drain, only to be replaced by a lost, vacant look.

"And what if I do?" Marilyn's voice sounded hollow.

"Is he all right?"

Slowly, Marilyn nodded.

"Where is he?"

Marilyn pointed with her eyes and forehead toward the ceiling.

Mary followed her glance. "In the attic," she said. "Is that where you had him earlier this week when I was here?"

Marilyn nodded.

"How did you do it?"

"When I stayed at your house, while you were at work, I got Timmy to be my friend. He trusted me because I lived with you."

"He never said anything to Susan or me."

"It was our secret." Marilyn smiled a dry, empty smile. "He knew he wasn't suppose to tell because it would spoil the surprise."

The more Marilyn explained, the tighter the knot became in Mary's stomach. Her daughter had worked out every detail. It was going to be just like before, except that this time Mary would intervene. "I can't let you keep Timmy. I'm going to go up there, bring him down, and take him home."

Marilyn shrugged. "He won't go."

"Why not?"

"He thinks his Mama is coming here."

"She's already here."

A wild, unharnessed look crossed Marilyn's eyes. Then as quickly as it came, it was gone. "She'll never get him back."

Marilyn's attitude surrounded Mary with fear. She had to keep her daughter talking. Keep her away from Timmy. "Why don't we go in and sit down?" Mary took a step toward the living room.

"Don't need to do that. We're fine here." Marilyn blocked the doorway, her hands still behind her back.

Mary backed up. "All right. This is fine right here." Her eyes darted from object to object, her mind scrambled with doubts. "I don't understand how you pulled it off."

"It was simple. A little bit of make-up, a bottle of hair tint, and hair re-styled to match Susan's. Didn't everyone always say that Susan and I could pass for twins if only our hair was the same color?"

Mary nodded.

"That's because we had the same daddy, huh, Mommy?"

Mary remained quiet.

"Susan's daddy was my daddy too. Wasn't he?"

Mary looked down.

"It doesn't matter. I've known it all along." She shrugged as though dismissing the idea.

"I watched Susan's house every morning from your kitchen window. Did you know that?"

Mary shook her head.

"Well, I did. Then I noticed she had a headache—I could tell by the way she kept rubbing her forehead, and she was still wearing her robe. So I knew she wasn't going to work. That was the day I'd been waiting for." Marilyn smiled, obviously pleased with herself. "Once I got to the daycare center, all I had to do was keep enough distance between the people at the daycare and me. I told them my headache might mean the coming of a cold and I didn't want them to get sick."

"But how could you fool Timmy?"

"I didn't have to. He knew I was coming for him sometime. We were going to surprise Mommy. It was all a game to him."

Marilyn's lips curved into a sadistic smile, an action which left Mary feeling cold. Forcing some calmness into her voice she said, "Marilyn, listen—"

"No, Mother, you listen," she took a step forward, "because I am through listening." From behind her she drew a butcher knife.

Chapter Thirty-Three

By the time Susan returned to her car, the fury of the storm had subsided, and all that was left was the slow steady drizzle which resembled strings hanging from the sky.

As she got into her car, her mind centered on Marilyn. Susan could still see her standing at the edge of the cliff. Laughing. The wind caressing her blond hair—

Blond hair.

Susan reached up and ran her fingers though her own brown hair. She had always been a brunette. It was Marilyn who was the blond. This constant memory of blond hair should have made her realize that she was reliving the past by seeing it from Marilyn's point of view. But what had driven her to remember it that way?

She shook her head, started the engine, and reached up to re-adjust the mirror. An unexpected sound of thunder bellowing in anger in the far distance startled her, and she moved the mirror in such a position that she was staring at herself.

She gasped as a thought flashed through her mind: Marilyn and Susan were standing in front of a bedroom mirror. Marilyn's head slowly turned to stare at Susan, and she said, "If your hair was blond like mine, we could pass as twins. Let's do that. From now on we'll be twins."

Twins.

She wished she could tell Bronson what she'd remembered. She needed to get to a telephone booth. She started the car, stepped on the accelerator, and sped off. Less than half-an-hour later, Susan could see the Happy Days Inn parking lot. She stopped across the street from the motel and ran to the public phone booth. Her fingers nervously tapped on the side of her leg as she waited to be connected with Bronson.

"I'm sorry, but Detective Bronson isn't available. Can I leave him a message?" came a voice over the phone.

"This is Susan Haynes. Please have him call me immediately. He can reach me at Happy Days Inn in Pine Basin, New Mexico. Also, please tell him to search for Marilyn, uh, Marilyn...Logan! Ask him to please find anything he can about her."

Susan hung up the phone. She felt as though thousands of needle-fine points were being shoved into her. Marilyn. Mary's daughter...

They had been so close back then, up until that moment at the cliff...

* * * *

At first Susan tried to pick up Kelly and take her back to her house. But when she realized this was impossible, she scurried back up the cliff, then down the path. She ran in a state of horror, her mind shutting out the monstrous trees whose raw limbs reach out and grabbed her and scratched her. The wind howled, the sky darkened. The blackness descended on Susan, threatening to imprison her.

"Suuusan! Wait!" It was Marilyn calling out to her. It was Death summoning her.

Susan pushed herself forward, her side aching. Her face streaked with tears and blood. She stumbled and lost her balance. She heard a very distinct thump as her head made contact with the ground. For a moment she felt disoriented.

Behind her, she heard Marilyn tease, "Suuusan! Oh, Susan. I'm catching up."

Desperately, Susan tried to stand up, but as she did, the world around her started to spin at great speed. Background noises became ripples in the air, gradually disappearing like waves. She was aware of footsteps shifting quietly around her. She closed her eyes and gave in to the surrounding darkness.

* * * *

Susan slowly opened her eyes. She wasn't alone. She was in a bedroom, but not her own. The face before her was familiar. Blond hair. Huge, twinkling brown eyes. Crooked grin, almost sadistic. Evil.

Marilyn!

Susan screamed.

Gentle hands pushed her back down. Susan hadn't been aware that she had tried to get up until Mary made her lay back down.

"Hush," Mary said. "You are perfectly safe now."

"K-k-kelly," Susan murmured.

"I know. I know," Mary comforted. "It was a tragic accident."

"No accident."

"Don't ever say that!" Mary's stern voice sent a chill through Susan's body. "They'll take you away and lock you up forever. Have you ever seen a prison? It's dark and smelly. Filled with rats. And roaches."

Darkness filled Susan's mind. Its shadows, like wispy smoke, crept all around. Susan shivered and tried to shut the image out.

"Would you like to be put in a place like that?"

Susan held her breath and shook her head. "I didn't do it. Mari—"

"You mean you didn't mean to do it."

"No! I tried to help—"

"Susan, listen to me." Mary grabbed Susan by the shoulders and shook her.

Susan felt her throat tighten with shock. She bit her lip to keep from crying out.

Mary tightened her grip on Susan. "Your dress was covered with blood. Kelly's blood. You came here in a state of hysterics, screaming and yelling how you had pushed Kelly. Don't you remember doing that?"

Susan thought, no that wasn't right. She shook her head.

From under the bed, Mary retrieved Susan's soiled dress and shoved it into her face. "See? This is your dress. It's filled with Kelly's blood. Do you know why? Because you killed Kelly."

"No," she whispered. "It wasn't like that." How could she convince her?

Mary released Susan. "That's fine, Susan, but I want you to know that I have your father's permission to keep you here as long as I see fit. The way I see it, you can't get well until you admit you killed Kelly."

Susan looked longingly out the window, toward the direction of her house. "Daddy?"

"He won't come, Susan. He'll never come. Not until you tell the truth."

"I'm telling the truth." She held back a sob. "I swear, I am."

"Do you know what happens to little girls who lie? They're punished."

She yanked Susan out of bed and dragged her toward the kitchen. Susan attempted to wiggle her way out of Mary's grasp, but Mary was much too strong for her. Mary opened the cellar door. "You're going to stay down there until you can admit that you cold-heartedly killed Kelly." She pushed her down the stairs and Susan tumbled to the bottom.

For a long time, Susan remained perfectly still. She was squatting, her arms wrapped around her legs, her head resting on her knees. She felt unbelievably cold. And lonely.

It was so dark. So very dark. She had always known that Evil lived in dark corners. The more she stared at the darkness, the more she was sure she could see it. Like a vaporous cloud, it flowed away from the corner and toward her. Susan held her breath. Maybe it couldn't see her in the dark. But then she heard it hiss like a snake, and she knew it was coming for her. It was angry at her for hiding. It hovered just above her, sending out its wispy smoke to search for her, stopping only when it found her. She felt icy black fingers scratching their way through her skin, trying to reach her, to make her a part of the darkness.

Susan screamed and sprang up. The stairs were here somewhere. She had to get away from the darkness. She stumbled and fell, but even then, she continued to push forward until, mercifully, she felt what she was sure were the steps. Reverting to all fours, she began to climb them. Once, she stopped to catch her breath, but as quickly as possible she continued to push on forward. She knew that the evil was watching and waiting for her to come back to the bottom.

Finally she found what she had been searching for: the cellar door. She fumbled around until she located the knob. She desperately twisted it. It was locked from the outside.

Susan pounded on the door. "Please, let me out. The darkness is here. It's going to get me. Please, open the door. It's so dark in here." She pounded until she felt blood seeping from her knuckles.

Behind her, the darkness softly laughed, mocking her terror.

Susan covered her mouth with her hands and tasted her blood.

* * * *

Susan stared at her hands. The wrinkles which come with age had started to creep in. Her hands were no longer the hands of her youth. They were no longer little girl hands. They were no longer covered with blood.

Her suppressed childhood memories crawled over her, making her feel overwhelmingly helpless. She ran back to the motel room and locked the door behind her.

She sat on the bed.

The cellar had been so cold. So damp. Creepy things lurked in there. They were coming to get her for killing Kelly.

Susan crawled to the corner of her bed, to the place where the two walls met. She pulled her legs up against her chest and wrapped her arms around them.

Staring vacantly ahead, she began to rock.

Chapter Thirty-Four

In one quick slash, Marilyn opened Mary's abdomen. The knife passed through her flesh as lightly as butter. It left Mary feeling a dull, burning sensation, and she knew she had no chance. The best she could do was hold herself together as her life blood seeped through her fingers and onto the floor.

"Oh, Mama, look at the mess you're making. I have a lot of things to do. I don't have time to clean up now." Marilyn turned her mother around and started pushing her. "Come on, hurry. Let's go."

Mary, too weak to resist, did as Marilyn told her. Folded over in pain, she followed Marilyn even though she knew she was the lamb being led to slaughter. At this point, she didn't care. All she wanted was for this unbearable pain to stop.

They reached the cellar door, and Mary whimpered like a child. She knew what was coming. She lowered her head and closed her eyes. Terror and weakness rooted her to the spot. She heard Marilyn open the cellar door. A mighty shove sent her rolling down the dark steps. Blinding lights exploded in her abdomen and brain. She stopped rolling and lay sprawled on the cold floor.

Her first instinct was to climb up the stairs. The cellar door was open and light was filtering in.

She dragged herself toward the foot of the stairs. Her pain intensified and peaked. Her struggles became a graceful ballet of death. She stopped.

It'd be best to go away from the light and head toward the darkness of the cellar. Then, when her body was found, maybe Susan would understand.

"I'm sorry, Susan," Mary said aloud even though it pained her to speak. She tightened herself into a little ball in an effort to protect herself against her mounting fears.

"Is Susan still here, Mommy?"

Startled, Mary shook herself. She hadn't realized Marilyn was there with her. "No, Marilyn, she's not here."

"Then why are you talking to her?"

"I was hoping that somehow she understood."

"Understood what?"

"That we know that what we did was wrong. We shouldn't have locked her up."

There was a long pause, and Mary wondered if Marilyn had left. She was about to call for her when Marilyn spoke. "Why did you do it?"

"To protect you, Marilyn—to force her to believe she killed Kelly."

"Kelly's evil."

It disturbed Mary how Marilyn referred to Kelly as though she was still alive. "No, she wasn't."

"She wants to take Susan away from me."

Mary closed her eyes, forcing her pain, her anguish to leave her. Somehow she had to make Marilyn understand. "Kelly's dead."

"No, Mommy. She's up in the attic."

"That's Timmy, and you must return him—unharmed—to Susan."

"I can't. I must show her the Secret Place."

"No, Marilyn, please don't do that. Too many people have already been hurt. Listen to me." A stab of pain shot through her body. "There isn't much time left, and you've got to understand. Kelly is dead."

"What about Susan's father—my father?"

"He's dead."

Marilyn moved away from the darkness and sat on the steps, so that now Mary could see her perfectly. "I know," she said. "I used to admire him so much, but not any more. Do you know why?"

"No, Marilyn, tell me why." Anything to keep her away from Timmy.

"Because he always defended Susan, but when she needed him the most—all those weeks she was locked in our cellar—he never came to visit her."

"That's because he didn't know she was locked away. He thought she had really killed Kelly, gone into shock, and was in a coma." Mary paused to take a deep breath. The pain was unbearable, and it was hard to keep the conversation going. But she had to try. She owed Susan at least that much. "Martin was pretty messed up himself. He couldn't handle seeing his daughter that way. He knew I was a registered nurse, and he was sure I was taking very good care of her."

"But you weren't." Marilyn fidgeted with a strand of her hair.

"No, I—we—locked her up in the cellar. Do you remember doing that? And, Marilyn, I'm responsible for his death. He loved me and I used his love to betray him. I told him—we told him—that Susan was in a coma. We said we were taking very good care of her. Instead, we kept her locked up here in the cellar."

Marilyn didn't answer.

"Listen, Marilyn, you've got to remember. If you can remember that, then you've got to realize that that's not Kelly up there. That's Timmy, not Kelly.

Kelly's dead. You killed Kelly."

"This is boring, Mommy. I'm going to go get Kelly and show her the Secret Place."

"No! Marilyn, wait. Please, come back. I'm dying. Stay with me." Mary heard her daughter giggle as she climbed the stairs.

With a sinking sensation, Mary listened to her daughter's footsteps heading toward the attic. She could distinctly hear Marilyn gently calling Kelly's name.

Chapter Thirty-Five

Just like before, the darkness came. Slowly, stealthily, smothering her.

Susan wrapped her arms tightly around her drawn up legs. Black fingers tapped at her mind, reminding her of another time, a time she didn't want to relive. There must be a place she could go to escape these memories.

There was.

The darkness would protect her. She would go toward its safety.

Something held her back. A voice. Someone was calling her. But this voice was so far away, and the darkness—the safety—led directly opposite the voice's direction.

"Suuusan!"

Should she go to the voice?

"Come back to me, Susan."

She looked at the darkness. It welcomed her.

"Susan, snap out of it!"

Someone grabbed her by the shoulders and shook her, but not really. It was more like she was outside this person named "Susan," and she was watching, feeling no particular emotion other than wanting to go to the darkness.

"Think of Timmy!" the voice said.

Timmy? But the darkness—

Timmy!

It was easy to enter the darkness and this time not leave its security.

TIMMY!

Susan screamed and she felt someone hug her tightly.

"It's okay, Susan. You're okay now." It was Bronson. "Everything is okay now." He squeezed her tightly and gently rocked her, like a mother comforting her child.

Giant waves of relief flooded Susan. Every nerve in her body tingled. She had confronted her past, and she'd won, thanks to Bronson. He was right. It was going to be okay. She nodded, like an idiot.

"You remembered it all, huh?" Bronson asked, still rocking her.

Susan continued to nod.

"Wanna tell me about it?"

Susan pulled back from Bronson's embrace, drew in a breath, and began her narration. Often she had to stop, taking the time to breathe deeply in order to calm down. At times, she spoke quickly and more to herself than Bronson as though seeking reassurance of its reality.

She told him about Kelly and how Mary had locked her in the cellar until she was convinced that she had killed Kelly. Only then, was she allowed to go home.

"Excuse me, Susan, for interrupting," Bronson said as he glanced at his notes. "But wouldn't it be obvious to assume that once you went home, you'd slowly start comin' out of your shell?"

"I think I was, but the progress was so slow I don't think Daddy ever noticed it."

"Why's that?"

"He seemed so preoccupied. At that time, I

didn't know why, but now I know. He was getting ready to institutionalize me. Then one day he called for both Mary and me..."

* * * *

Martin sat Susan on his lap and wrapped his arm around her. She could feel him trembling.

"Promise me, Mary, that no matter what happens, you'll always take care of my little Susan."

Mary's forehead wrinkled with concern. "Of course," she cautiously answered, "but what makes you think that anything is going to happen?"

Martin didn't answer, but instead stared at his daughter, squeezed her tightly, and handed her to Mary. With his eyes, he signaled for Mary and Susan to leave.

Holding onto Susan's hand, Mary led her out, and closed the office door behind them. Her hand was still on the doorknob when the explosion of a gun reverberated throughout the house.

Mary's eyes popped opened. "Oh God, no!" She dropped Susan's hand and yanked the door open.

Blood was splattered on the wall, the carpet, the furniture. Martin's body quivered a couple of times then was still. He had slumped backwards in his large swivel chair. In the place where his face should have been, there was only a hole held together by pieces of flesh.

Susan shook violently. Daddy! Daddy shot himself. It was an accident. It had to be. If it wasn't, that meant...

That meant...

Slowly, Susan nodded as she began to understand. Mary had been right. She was an evil child. First she had killed Kelly—hadn't she?—and now, she had killed Daddy just as surely as if she had pulled the trigger herself.

Daddy was no more.

And neither should she be.

She'd crawl somewhere deep inside herself where she couldn't harm anyone anymore. She was, after all, evil.

Evil...

* * * *

"It took me over ten years," Susan gasped for air, "before I was functional again." She fought the feeling that she was evil. She shook herself.

"That's a very long time," Bronson said as he snapped his spiral notebook shut. "But it's over now."

"It's not over until I have Timmy back."

"You feel Marilyn has him?" It was more of a statement than a question.

"I'm sure of it," Susan said, "just as I am sure he's still alive."

"How do you know this?"

"Because I know Marilyn. She plans to keep him safe until his birthday."

"Which is?"

"Tomorrow."

"In that case, let's go get Timmy right now," Bronson said.

Chapter Thirty-Six

Bronson glanced at the notes he had scribbled in his spiral notebook. He snapped it and looked up at Susan. "Mary is here in Pine Basin," he said. "She left the day after you did."

Susan flopped down on the bed. "Damn! I was hoping she'd tell us where to find Marilyn. Now what?"

"Now we go talk to the motel owner."

An inquisitive look crossed Susan's face. "I don't understand."

"Think about it, Susan. Do you really expect me to believe that you stopped here in this run-down motel because you're trying to save a couple of bucks?"

Susan shook her head. "I'm not quite sure why I did stop here."

"I am," Bronson said. "You were following your instincts which told you that either you know the motel owner, or you know he knows something. Let's go find out which it is." He reached for Susan's hand and helped her up.

Mr. Tom, the motel's owner, was busy working the crossword puzzle in the newspaper. "Something I can do for you?" he asked without looking up.

Susan glanced at Bronson for reassurance, then said, "I was wondering if you could direct us to—"

"Pine Ranch," Mr. Tom said as he made an entry on the puzzle.

"I beg your pardon?" Bronson said.

"Marilyn. You did want to see Marilyn." This time he did look up at them.

"Why do you say that?" Bronson asked.

"I just can't see Miss Sue Haynes coming over here and not visiting Marilyn. They were the Bobbsey twins. Always together—those two. That is until that tragic accident." He stared at Bronson. "Did you hear about that? A little girl—let's see, what was her name? Oh, yeah, Kelly something or the other—she fell to her death pretty close to where Susan used to live."

He turned to Susan, "Shortly after she died, you disappeared. Rumor has it that you saw her jump and you, uh, couldn't handle it. So you went away. Is that true?"

"You know, you should have been a detective," Bronson said. "You're pretty good at this. Maybe you could help us."

Tom eyed him suspiciously. "Help? How?"

"We need some information about Marilyn. Does she live here in Pine Basin?"

"Yep. She lives in her old house." He pointed at Susan. "After her father's untimely death, the house remained empty for a couple of months. Then Marilyn moved in. Everyone in town, including me, thought it was pretty good idea. I mean, after all, Marilyn was almost family and Martin had no one else. But even though she's been living there for a long time, she hasn't changed a thing. The place, from what I understand, is still under Susan's name.

* * * *

As Susan sped down the highway, her stomach felt as if she had swallowed a live coal that was burning her insides. What if she was wrong? What if Marilyn didn't have Timmy?

"Sorry about not drivin'," Bronson said interrupting Susan's thoughts, "but I hate to drive. Did you know that?"

Susan nodded, stepped all the way down on the accelerator, and watched the needle climb to seventy-three.

"Better slow down," Bronson said holding on to the door handle. "You're driving with a policeman, and I'm allowed to give speeding tickets. You did know that, didn't you?"

Susan ignored him and Bronson shrugged. "I'm not quite sure why you think Timmy's safe only until his birthday."

The memory hit Susan like a physical pain. "It all began with my birthday party," she began to explain.

* * * *

The playroom at Pine Ranch was decorated with bright, happy streamers, balloons of all sizes and shapes, and a life-size cardboard clown juggling brightly colored balls which spelled out:
H-A-P-P-Y B-I-R-T-H-D-A-Y.

It promised to be a great party. The only thing that would make it more perfect was if Susan and Kelly spent a little time alone. Marilyn was always with them. Susan was beginning to consider Marilyn a chaperon instead of a friend. Just this once, Susan wanted to enjoy Kelly's company without Marilyn's interference.

Susan would never consider having a party and not inviting Marilyn. But she could ask Kelly to come at least two hours early. Kelly seemed excited at the thought, but at the same time, somewhat hesitant.

An hour before the party was scheduled to start, Kelly still hadn't shown up. Susan called her and begged her to come. Fifteen minutes later, Kelly arrived. Susan was glad to see her. She reached for her hand. "Come," she said. "Let me show you my new Barbie clothes. They're up in my room."

Susan led her up the stairs and closed her bedroom door. As they glanced at all the clothes, they started daydreaming about when and where they could wear such attractive and expensive clothes. Their active imaginations gave them a case of the giggles.

Suddenly, the bedroom door swung open. Marilyn stood in the doorway, her face taut with rage. "Don't ever leave me out again!" Hostility seethed through each of Marilyn's pores.

"Marilyn! I didn't—we didn't," Susan quickly said.

"She was just showing me her new—"

"I don't care what she was showing you. What matters is that you left me out, and no one leaves me out. Is that understood?" She spoke with a venomous tone. "Get out, Kelly. The party is downstairs. You don't belong up here."

Susan started to protest, but at the last moment she hesitated. Kelly mumbled, "Sorry," as she walked past Marilyn.

As soon as Kelly left, Marilyn's features softened. "I want us to make a promise to each other," she said as she stepped into the bedroom and sat on the edge of the bed. "I want you to promise me that you will never love anyone more than me. And I promise that I'll never love anyone more than you. Okay?"

In spite of the way Marilyn had just treated Kelly, Susan still felt thrilled and honored. Eagerly, Susan nodded.

"Good." Marilyn smiled. "We're like blood sisters now. It'll always be just you and me and no one will ever come between us. I'll make sure of that."

* * * *

"We sealed our special bond on that day. No matter what—we promised each other—this bond would tie us through eternity," Susan said and Bronson nodded, signifying he had heard.

Susan continued, "Now I understand why she felt she had to kill Kelly. She did it for me. She felt that I might care more for Kelly than her. Maybe I could have saved Kelly. All I had to do was re-assure Marilyn that no one was more important than she."

No one.

Did she now think Timmy was more important than she? Anxiety ate away at Susan as she remembered Marilyn's words: Just you and me and no one will ever come between us.

Stop it! Susan ordered herself. This is different. We were kids then with no thoughts of having children of our own.

—no one will ever come between us.

Susan floored the accelerator again. From where she was, she could see the Pine Basin Ranch cut-off. They were almost there.

—no one will ever—

Susan slowed down, made the turn, and followed the bumpy road leading to Pine Ranch.

—ever—

Two miles later, Susan brought the car to a halt at the top of the road, a place she knew where they couldn't possibly be seen from the house. "It's down there," she said. "You can see it if you stand at the edge of the road."

Bronson opened the car door but didn't get out. "I'm gonna ask you to do the hardest thing in your life." He swung his legs out. "I want you to stay here in the car and wait for me."

"But..."

"If Timmy and Marilyn are there, and if either of them see you, you could, without meaning to, royally screw things up."

Reluctantly, Susan agreed.

Chapter Thirty-Seven

From the top of the hill, Susan stared at her house. The longer she stood there, the more her confidence drained from her like water from a leaky glass. It'd been ten minutes, actually eleven minutes and twenty-three seconds—she was counting—since Bronson had been swallowed by the thick forest below her. What could possibly be taking him so long? Maybe he needed help.

Her sense of foreboding deepened and groping haphazardly like a blind person in a maze, she worked her way down the hill toward her house.

She dashed from behind one tree to the other, always keeping the pines between her and the house.

She had stopped to catch her breath when she saw the front door open. Bronson stepped out and looked up the hill where the car was. He signaled for Susan to come down, then stepped back inside. With a new-found, savage ferocity, Susan rushed the rest of the way down the cliff, her eyes focused solely on the mansion below her. Several times she lost her balance and almost fell, but she didn't hesitate. She pushed on forward. The lump she felt in her throat made it impossible to swallow. Even though it was not more than five minutes later when Susan reached the house, she felt that hours had passed.

For a full second, Susan stopped. Bronson was there to meet her. She tried to read his face, but she couldn't make out anything. "Well?"

"Timmy's not here," he said, "but the evidence says he was. There are toys, which I assume belong to him." He looked away and swallowed hard. He shifted position. "There's more."

Susan held her breath.

"Mary is in there, Susan."

"And?"

"She's dead."

Susan gasped. "Dead? How?"

"Murdered."

"Oh God!" She attempted to run inside the house.

Bronson stopped her. "You can't go in there."

"Why not? It's my house."

"It's also the scene of a crime. You might destroy some evidence."

"Where's...Mary?"

"In the cellar."

"I won't go near the cellar. But I have to get to the playroom, upstairs."

"Why?"

"I have to see it. There might be something in there. I can't explain it. I just know I've got to go in there."

Bronson considered this for a moment, then said, "Let's go." He led her inside the house.

She saw with sudden fright the pools of semi-dried blood leading to the cellar. She backed away a pace and put her hand to her throat. She could feel its pulse throbbing beneath her fingers. She forced herself to look away from the blood. She turned and ran up the stairs.

The door to the playroom was closed but not locked. Feeling as though the door would come to life, Susan braced herself and pushed it open. She didn't know what she was expecting to see, but she certainly wasn't prepared for what she did find. Each individual fragment registered on her mind like a movie playing in slow motion.

The first thing that froze her blood was the life-size cardboard clown juggling the balls which spelled out H-A-P-P-Y B-I-R-T-H-D-A-Y. Its silhouette projected starkly on the wall.

Underneath the clown rested some unopened presents. Streamers and balloons decorated the ceiling. Some toys, all new, remained scattered along the floor. A half-eaten cake and an empty bowl of punch supported her theory that there had been a recent party.

With growing apprehension, Susan stared at each abhorring detail. Marilyn had decorated the room the same way it had been on that night when she and Marilyn had sealed their bond.

Behind her, Bronson asked, "Does it mean anything to you?"

Susan nodded. "On my birthday, Marilyn and I made that pledge. Looking back on it now, that's probably the same day she planned to kill Kelly." She stared at the clown—that stupid clown. "They say history repeats itself."

"Yes, Ma'am, I've heard the expression."

"What bothers me is that Marilyn already celebrated Timmy's birthday. Why did she do that? His birthday's not until tomorrow." Susan's muscles knotted, rocklike.

"Maybe Mary's arrival forced her to move up his birthday."

"Could be." She fought the overwhelming urge to scream hysterically. "Or maybe she did it to get it out of the way. She's now ready..." she bit her lip, "ready to kill him. Or has she...already done so?" She choked on her emotions. She could hear the wailing of the approaching police sirens. The noise sent her pulse racing.

"We'll get them to help us look for Timmy." Bronson went down the stairs to go meet them.

"I don't have time to wait," she said, but Bronson didn't hear her. He immediately busied himself showing the policemen the body.

Susan tried to wait, tried to be patient, but at this very minute, Marilyn could be dragging Timmy to the Secret Place. The thought fueled her panic and increased her pace as she stormed out of the house.

Chapter Thirty-Eight

In spite of the fact that the trail was often partially obstructed by brush, Susan sped through the forest like a wild animal in search of its prey. It wasn't long before she was breathing hard. She felt a stitch in her side, but she ignored it. Her body ached for a place to rest, but she kept pushing forward. Often she scraped her arms and legs, but she didn't care. All she knew was that she had to reach the Secret Place as soon as possible. She prayed she wouldn't be too late.

Oh, Timmy, Susan thought. Please hold on. Just a little longer. I'm coming, honey. Mommy is finally coming.

In her hurry, Susan failed to see the protruding rock. As she tripped, she instinctively placed her arms in front of her, breaking the fall. She landed on her hands and knees. Pain from her left leg shot up through her body as she rose. Susan wiped the blood oozing from a bad wound on her knee and proceeded to make her way through the hill as quickly as possible.

Her leg protested, but Susan continued to climb until she reached the crest of the hill. She was halfway there.

Out of necessity, she stopped for a second. The

forest, she noticed, had become unbearably silent, and its stillness filled Susan with dread. Even the crickets had ceased their chirping. It was as if all the creatures in the forest knew that there was some type of predator among them.

Susan pushed on. Faster.

By now her legs were bruised and tender, and each step rang out the pain—the fear—in her. The wind chilled her tear-stained face. Trying to catch her breath, Susan wrapped her arm around a pine tree. She stared at the path. In several places the trees blocked the sunlight causing the darkness to fill her with apprehension. She continued to study the trail until she found what she was looking for. A stump sat twenty, thirty feet in front of her. If she stood on its top, she would have a clear view of the Secret Place.

Her mind screamed, Hurry! Run! But fear of discovering the truth made her legs seem like they had become separate entities. Susan stood frozen, staring directly in front of her. Somewhere from below her, she could hear faint noises: the rustling of leaves or perhaps the murmur of voices. The sounds urged her to move. As though someone had suddenly pressed the on button, she darted forward, and in less than a minute, she was standing on top of the stump looking down.

Oh, God, they were there.

Timmy was standing at the end of the fallen tree. Marilyn, her back to Susan, was obviously encouraging him to move forward. She held something shiny beside her. Susan focused her attention on Marilyn's hands. She was holding a large kitchen knife.

Susan opened her mouth to scream, but she caught herself in time. She stifled the noise. It wouldn't be wise to let them know she was here. It might cause Marilyn to react drastically.

As frightening as the thought was, she knew Timmy was safer standing on that fallen tree than if he was standing next to Marilyn. If he didn't do as she said, Susan knew Marilyn wouldn't hesitate to stab him.

As Susan stood helplessly staring, Marilyn grabbed Timmy by both shoulders and made him stand on top of the tree trunk. The fear Susan felt was physical. There was an acidic taste in her mouth, a crawling sensation in her stomach. Susan covered her mouth as she saw Marilyn place the knife by Timmy's throat. His body went rigid with fear.

"No! No! No!" Susan repeatedly sobbed. The words seemed to flutter around her like frightened birds.

For one eternal second Timmy glanced up, toward Susan. His young, tender face was chiseled with fear, his eyes begging for help. Then, they turned to stare back at Marilyn. She withdrew the knife, and Timmy took a hesitant step forward.

In that instant, Susan knew she had to reach the bottom as soon as possible. Once she had joined them, she would treat it like a game. She wouldn't frighten Marilyn. She wouldn't frighten Timmy. Susan's heart thumped wildly and her stomach turned as she leaped off the stump.

She tried to land and run at the same time. But instead, she crumbled to the ground like a half-empty sack of flour. Susan landed on her side, and for a fraction of a second, she didn't know if she should push forward or sideways to get up. Her body jerked and there were pine trees all around her. The sky was where her feet should be. The ground was to her right, left, above, and below her, and she realized she was tumbling down the hill.

In one of those rolls—Susan didn't know which, they all seemed the same—she felt a searing pain as her head hit the ground.

After what must have been a few seconds of uncontrolled rolling and sliding down the hill, Susan's body came to rest. The throbbing pain made her grab the back of her head. It felt damp and warm. She brought her hand down and stared at it. It was smeared with blood.

Susan looked up. Timmy, screaming and trembling with fear, was a quarter of the way out on the log. He seemed unaware of his mother's arrival, but Marilyn had spotted her. As though moving in slow motion, she turned to stare at Susan.

Susan opened her mouth to form the name Timmy, but nothing came out. Her vision blurred, but she refused to give up. She dragged herself a foot, and the world around her spun wildly.

No! I must go on.

She tried to stand up but she was so dizzy, she was unable to. She crawled, two, three more feet. Her anger, her frustrations gave her the strength to carry on.

In the far distance Timmy cried, "No, please, I don't want to go. Don't make me go."

Susan's fingers curved, trying to reach out to Timmy. She heard Marilyn's laughter pealing through the air, filling the evening with a freezing chill.

The blackness around Susan enveloped her.

Chapter Thirty-Nine

A bolt of agony brought Susan back to consciousness. Her entire left side cried out in pain. Her hair was matted with blood and dirt.

She opened her eyes and tried to focus. All she saw was a blur. She shut her eyes tightly, then reopened them. Gradually, the blur began to take shape as general outlines of her surroundings. The details, however, remained out of focus. With a terrifying sense of déjà vu, Susan's first thought was of Timmy. Panic choked her. She tried to get up, but all she managed to do was raise her head.

"You shouldn't have come, you know," a voice behind Susan said.

Susan twisted her head and saw Marilyn sitting on a large rock approximately ten feet away. Using the edge of a stick, she was aggravating the ants.

Marilyn said, "It's too bad you're here." She threw the stick away, stood up, and walked slowly toward Susan, stopping when she neared her side.

"Timmy?" Susan asked, holding her breath in anticipation.

"Why did you come?"

"Timmy. I have to see him. Where is he?"

There was no answer.

"Please, Marilyn, tell me. Where is he?"

Marilyn reached down and picked up the ten-inch kitchen knife Susan had seen before. It had been sticking out of the ground no more than two feet away from Susan's head. She wished she had known it was within her reach, but now it was too late.

Marilyn swung the knife threateningly, causing the sun's rays to make its deadly edge glint dangerously. Its sharp glare momentarily blinded Susan, filling her with terror. She forced down her fear. Her need to know about Timmy's safety overrode her concern for personal safety.

Using her elbows to raise her upper body, Susan tried to sit up. Immediately Marilyn placed the knife dangerously close to Susan's face. "Uh-uh, uh-uh." The second uh-uh was an octave higher. "I wouldn't do that if I were you."

Susan lay back down, rolling onto her side. Her eyes continued to frantically search for Timmy. All she saw were trees, boulders, and a ground scattered with all the debris of a forest. "Please, tell me where he is," she begged.

"Who?"

"Timmy."

"Dead."

The answer hit her like a locomotive. No, it wasn't true.

It couldn't be true.

Any second now Timmy would come running out from behind a tree. "I tricked you, Mommy. I tricked you." Susan strained to look at the trees around her. Which one was it?

Oh, hurry, Timmy. Come out.

Come out.

I want to see you.

Hold you.

I want—

—to scream. To let it out. I want to let go of the pain but I can't. Not now. Not ever.

Feeling a terrible sense of emptiness, Susan rolled her face to the side. She had lost everything. Her eyes filled with tears and she closed them, trying to keep the anguish locked inside.

No!

She would not accept this answer. No one would ever convince her that Timmy was dead until she actually saw his body. Susan felt the rage build within her. Suddenly she hated this woman who had once been her friend.

"No!" she screamed. A surge of adrenaline gave Susan the strength to bounce to her feet. She sprang toward Marilyn, catching her unaware.

Slashing wildly, Marilyn thrust the knife into Susan's left shoulder. Surprised that she had actually wounded Susan, Marilyn reacted quickly. She drew the knife back and pushed Susan down. "You don't listen, do you? You're just like everybody else."

Susan landed with a dull thud. She placed her right hand over her wounded shoulder and applied pressure.

Looking desperately around, she noticed a good-sized branch—one she should be able to easily swing with one arm. It would make an effective club. The problem was reaching it. Susan suppressed a moan and rolled toward it carefully. When she realized there was no reaction from Marilyn, she rolled again and closed her eyes. It was still out of reach.

Alert for any noises, Susan was curious when she heard what sounded like digging. Cautiously, she opened her eyes. Marilyn was sitting in the dirt, stabbing it over and over with the knife.

"She shouldn't have tried to interfere," Marilyn said, withdrawing the knife and wiping the blade on her jeans.

Marilyn stood up, turned and gave Susan her back. She was staring over the precipice.

Susan inched her way toward the limb. She hoped it was as sturdy as it looked.

"I killed her for us, you know," Marilyn said.

"Her?" Susan asked. Weren't they talking about Timmy?

Abruptly, Marilyn turned and Susan remained perfectly still. "Yes, her—Kelly. Who did you think we're talking about?" She threw her arms up in the air. "Really, sometimes you're so exasperating. Why, I..."

Her words became a continuous slur, like a record played at the wrong speed. What Marilyn was saying didn't make sense. She was obviously talking about the past. Had she forgotten about Timmy?

"What about Timmy?" Susan put as much force in her voice as she could.

"Who?" Marilyn's eyebrows furrowed. She moved over and stood beside Susan again.

Twice, Susan tried to sit up, and Marilyn reacted by squatting down and pressing the edge of the knife against the tip of Susan's nose. She let it rest there for a second or two, smiled, then gently pushed it in, causing a few drops of blood to well up. "You're staying right here," she said. "You won't ever leave me again. Remember our bond? You promised to love me above everyone else." She removed the blade and wiped the blood away from Susan's nose. "You're hurt. That's too bad."

Without moving her head, Susan's eyes darted, searching behind each bush, behind each tree. "Timmy!" she yelled. If only she could reach that limb. She stretched some more.

Marilyn sighed and stood up. "It really is a shame," she said. "She was halfway across that log when she lost her balance."

Halfway across? If Kelly had taken four or five more steps, she would have reached solid ground and safety.

"You should have seen her face," Marilyn continued. "Pure horror." She squealed like a toddler filled with delight. "You know what scared her the most?" She raised the knife in front of her. "This knife."

Knife?

"When she saw this blade pointing at her, she knew she had to cross that log," Marilyn continued. "She knew what I would do if she disobeyed me and refused to cross the log."

Marilyn didn't have a knife when she killed Kelly, Susan thought. Oh, Timmy. The tears gushed out of Susan's eyes like a faucet turned on full. I'm sorry, honey. Oh, Timmy.

Timmy.

Not caring anymore if Marilyn saw her, Susan inched her way toward the limb. Her fingertips touched it so that now all she needed to do was grab it.

Marilyn squinted and quickly went to her. "Uh-uh, little girl. None of that now." She kicked the limb away, bent down and slashed at Susan only inches away from her face. "She's dead and I killed her." She stood up and walked away.

Susan began to move forward again, but this time toward the edge. All thoughts of using the limb as a weapon vanished. All she wanted to do was to look over the precipice and reassure herself that her son was not there. An overwhelming urge to cradle Timmy just one more time over took her. She needed to hold him. Touch him.

Suddenly, Marilyn grabbed Susan's hair and pulled her back. Susan felt the metallic blade of the knife pushed against her throat. "You don't listen too good," Marilyn said. "I told you to stay. You're like everybody else. They all tell me they love me. Then they leave me."

Susan tried not to breathe, not to swallow. The blade was that close to her throat.

Marilyn continued, "You're just like Mama. She promised me she would always be there for me, then she forgets all about me. Instead all she is worried about is Timmy. So I killed her. What about you, Susan? You will never leave me. Will you?" She pressed the knife harder against Susan's throat, and a hairline cut appeared.

Susan's neck burned, but she didn't cry out.

"I thought you loved me. But you're just like everyone else. First, you get married, then you have a child. Each time you push me farther away, leaving me behind. Well, I won't be left behind. Not ever! Do you understand?" She jerked Susan's head further up, exposing her throat even more.

Susan closed her eyes and tried to raise her arms to protect herself, but she had no strength. The pain in her head, her shoulder, her heart rendered her useless. She sucked in her breath in anticipation.

Just as Susan prepared to die, she heard someone gently say, "Hi, Marilyn." The male voice sounded as though it was coming from a far away place. It was gentle, firm—and vaguely familiar.

"Don't do it, Marilyn," he said. "Listen to me. It's me, Martin. Martin McFields. Susan's father. Daddy."

Marilyn gasped and shoved away Susan's head. Blinding lights exploded in Susan's brain as her head bounced on the ground. Everything around her seemed to slow down, but, even as movement began to loose its speed, Susan writhed toward the source of the voice.

Was it really Daddy? No, logic told her. He's dead. Unable to bear the humiliation Susan had put him through, he had shot himself. He was dead because of her. And now someone was bringing him back alive. Who? And why? Susan looked toward the source. She saw a large, powerful man half-hidden within the shadows cast by the trees.

"It's Martin," he repeated. "Come to Martin, Marilyn. Come to Martin."

Marilyn's eyes were fixed on him. Her eyes watered, and in a voice which sounded very much like a little girl's, she whispered, "Martin? Is it really you?"

"Yes. It's me. Come here."

Marilyn took two steps toward him before abruptly stopping. "No, it can't be you," she said. "You're dead."

"No, Marilyn, I'm very much alive."

Marilyn remained perfectly still for a minute.

"Come, my little pussy-cat. Don't keep me waiting."

Marilyn gasped. "No one's called me that since Martin. Martin...oh, God, it's you! Where have you been?"

"Away. Thinking."

"About?"

The answer came almost as a whisper. "About us."

"And?"

"And I decided I need you back in my life. I can't live without you."

"Oh, Martin, sweet Martin. I've missed you!" She took several steps forward.

Immediately Susan recognized the opportunity. She gritted her teeth, keeping the pain locked in. Using all of the strength she could muster, she threw herself toward the club.

The noise startled Marilyn and shook her out of her trance. She turned to face Susan who stood ready to swing the discarded limb.

"Do you hate me that much?" Marilyn scowled. "Yes, I suppose you do. But it's not me you should hate. Hate him!" She pointed toward the voice in the woods. "Ask him what he did to me when I was a little girl. Maybe he'll tell you how he couldn't keep his filthy hands off me. I hated it. No, I..." Her voice cracked. "I liked it." Her tone was filled with bitterness. "And I hate myself for that."

Susan still held on to the limb, but the power of Marilyn's words weakened her grip.

"I went looking for him, wanting him to continue hurting me like he used to. He said it wasn't right what we were doing. But I couldn't help it. He got me hooked. I couldn't let go. I needed him."

Behind Marilyn, the man hiding in the trees started moving toward her, always keeping to the shadows. Susan noticed him and bit her tongue to keep from saying anything.

Marilyn continued, "He said it was over. He was afraid you'd find out. He chose you over me. So I set out to take you away from him. I thought it was over, that day in his study. But he didn't tell you or Mama anything, but I knew that eventually he would. The fool! He was feeling guilty and just had to confess, as though that would make everything okay.

"So that day in the study, I hid and waited. As soon as both of you left, I shot him. I thought the secret was safe, but Mama knew." She glared at Susan. "But you didn't. You thought it was suicide. But I killed him—just like I killed your son, and now I'm going to kill you!" With a wild look in her face, she raised her arm up high and clutching the knife, she bolted toward Susan.

Susan, holding the limb like a bat, swung as hard as she could. The impact of the branch against Marilyn's chest knocked the wind from her. Marilyn dropped to the ground. Immediately Susan discarded the limb as though it had burned her.

"Are you all right?"

Susan looked up. For the first time she noticed Bronson and, behind him, several uniformed policemen. Slowly Susan nodded. "That was you back there?"

Bronson nodded.

"How did you know?"

"Back there in your house, when I got there, Mary was still alive. That's why it took me so long to come out. She told me everything before she died."

Susan nodded.

"I'm sorry, Susan."

"Timmy?"

"I just got here myself."

Again Susan nodded and looked toward the precipice. Without any further hesitation, she raced toward it.

"Susan, no! Don't do it."

Susan heard Bronson's warning, but she ignored him. Instead, she held her breath and forced herself to look down.

There his body lay.

It had never looked so small. So fragile. His still body lay so peaceful, so calm, so still. Susan felt the overwhelming urge to climb down and lie beside him so that the two on them could sleep. Together. Forever.

Strong arms grabbed Susan a second before she felt her body go limp.

Epilogue

It was raining.

Not the torrential type that completely soaks you in less than a minute, but a gentle drizzle that fills the heart with memories.

When a drop fell on Susan's cheek, she tried to wipe it away, but found that her arms would not obey the simple command. They were like two lead pipes too heavy to move.

Another drop landed on Susan's upper lip and rolled down between her lips. Its bitter, salty flavor urged her to again attempt to move, but her efforts went unnoticed. She'd try a different approach. She focused all of her energy on forming a word—any word. Nothing happened. She tried again.

And again.

"Susan?"

She heard her name being called, but it had been whispered in such coarse dismay that she wasn't sure she had heard it at all.

Maybe if she opened her eyes, the confusion would end. She found that her eyes, like her arms, were useless. They seemed to be glued shut.

Fighting a wave of despair, somewhere in the back of her mind a tiny voice desperately urged her to listen to the voice calling out to her. "Go to it," it said. "There's nothing in here for you but darkness." She understood the voice. She'd been there before. A long time ago and then again, not so long ago. She was every place and nowhere.

Snap out of it, she ordered herself. you can do it.

Concentrate. Move your arms, legs. Anything. Try harder.

Concentrate.

You can do it.

"Doctor! She moved her fingers." Again that familiar voice. Yet so far away. Maybe if I move toward it...

"Susan, can you hear me?" The voice was nearer. More distinct.

She opened her eyes.

"She's awake, Doctor! SHE'S AWAKE!"

Doctor?

She felt disoriented. Where was she? Why was everything so blurry? She closed her eyes once again, and when she reopened them, the double images began to float into a clear picture. The first thing she saw was a window. Beyond it, a tree. A sparrow fluttered and flew away. Tiny buds filled the branches. Spring was at its birth.

But not in Susan's heart. Timmy was gone, and she sadly realized that she hadn't been able to save him. Her body screamed from all the aches and pains, but this did not compare to the hollowness she felt.

Oh, God. It can't be true. She felt tears form in her eyes.

Not my Timmy.

He's not gone. He can't be gone. It was all a bad dream. That's all.

I'll call for him and he'll come running. I'll be

able to cuddle him. I'll be able to...

She began to scream, a high, piercing wail that rose from deep within her heart.

"Susan! What's wrong? You're safe now. I'm here."

The smooth voice and reassuring tone calmed her. She turned and immediately recognized Jeff's tear stained face. She smiled when she realized that it had been his tears, not the rain, which had brought her back.

"Are you okay? How do you feel?" he asked.

She reached for her forehead and found it covered with bandages. Her head throbbed, but only as it should after the abuse it had received. She realized that perhaps those dreadful headaches would never return because she had at long last remembered her past. But at what price, she thought. Oh, Timmy, I miss you. In spite of the agony tearing at her, she attempted to smile. "I'm fine."

"Susan, Timmy—"

The door to the hospital room opened and a short, plump lady neatly dressed in a nurses' uniform stepped in. "Did someone scream?" Her face flushed with anxiety.

"I was just letting everyone know I was awake," Susan said. She had made up her mind to try to put her past behind her.

The nurse smiled and winked, obviously relieved. Then she turned to Jeff who was standing beside the bed, gently rubbing the back of Susan's hand.

"Welcome back, Mrs. Haynes," the nurse said, then turned to Jeff. "I need you to wait outside while the doctor examines your wife."

Jeff nodded but did not move.

The nurse seemed to understand Jeff's feelings but did not let that interfere with her job. She gently grasped his arm and began to walk him to the door. "I promise I'll call you just as soon as we're finished."

Jeff nodded and allowed himself to be led outside. A big smile was plastered on his face. At the door, he made a weak attempt to return to Susan's bedside, but the nurse pushed him into the hallway. "I promise," she said.

She closed the door and walked toward Susan.

"Where am I?" Susan asked.

"St. Joseph's." The nurse reached for Susan's arm and began to check her pulse.

"St. Joseph's?" Susan asked. "In Dallas?"

The nurse smiled and nodded.

"How long have I been here?" Susan asked.

"You were flown in Monday morning at your husband's request." The nurse retrieved Susan's chart from the foot of the bed and began to look at it.

"What's today?"

"Wednesday."

The door swung open and an elderly doctor, looking very business-like, walked in.

* * * *

As soon as Jeff stepped out of Susan's room, he spotted Bronson heading toward him. For a fraction of a second, Bronson's steps faltered, then he broke into a wide smile and stretched out his hand to greet Jeff. "Your face tells it all. Susan is going to be okay.'

Jeff nodded. "Thank you for all you've done, Detective—" Jeff looked at him. "What the heck is your first name anyway?"

"Harry," he answered, smiling.

"Thank you, Harry." Jeff smiled back. "One thing that puzzles me is how you knew that Susan needed rescuing."

"That's simple. It involved a lot of research and a little bit of luck," Harry said as he leaned against the wall and stared at the closed door which led to Susan's room. "A lot of records were destroyed or altered in order to keep us from ever provin' anything. But luckily for us, Mary's ex-husband called to tell me Mary had a daughter who didn't quite seem to be 'normal'—that was his word, not mine. I figured it was mighty strange that nobody had ever mentioned this person, so that set me on the trail which eventually led back to Susan and Pine Basin."

"Were you shocked to learn that Mary had a daughter?" Jeff asked.

"No, not really. In fact, it all made perfect sense to me. Gut instinct told me that Susan hadn't picked Timmy up at the daycare center. But I knew someone had, someone who strongly resembled her. I knew Mary couldn't have possibly done it, what with the age difference and all. But I felt that she knew something which she wasn't telling. A daughter fit in the picture just perfectly."

Jeff nodded and shrugged simultaneously. "It's a shame, though, that it turned out the way it did." He was quiet for a while, then added, "By the way, how's Marilyn?"

"Catatonic," Harry answered, "and I'd say that's a case of poetic justice."

Jeff sighed. "I suppose," he agreed. "Do you think she'll ever be okay?"

"I'm not a psychiatrist." Harry shrugged. "We'll just have to wait and see."

Jeff looked down the hallway and was quiet for a moment. Then he said, "May God forgive her and help her because I don't know if I ever will. I just can't get over Mary. I thought she really cared for us."

"I reckon she did, but like all mothers, her loyalty lay first with her own child."

"That reminds me, I'm going upstairs and preparing a very pleasant surprise for Susan."

"You didn't tell her?"

"I hardly got to speak two, three words to her before I was kicked out."

"Then hurry up, young man. That door might open any time now."

* * * *

A few minutes later, the door did open and the doctor and nurse stepped out, leaving Susan alone in the room. Harry looked down the hallway and noticed that Jeff still hadn't arrived. He decided to go on in without Jeff.

When Susan saw the detective standing in her doorway, she opened her arms in greeting. Harry slowly walked toward her. "Now, uh, Ma'am, my wife is mighty particular as to which ladies I should hug." His face although not quite red, was definitely a shade of pink. "Oh, well, I reckon she won't mind this time." He wrapped his arms around Susan. "Jeff should be right outside by now. Let me go check." He stepped out and saw him coming. "Yep, he's here," he said and closed the door.

"What...?" Susan looked at Harry.

"You'll see." His eyes lit up like bright, happy sparks in a dark room.

Unable to contain her curiosity, Susan was glad when she heard the knocking at her door.

"Come in," she quickly said straining her neck to see. For some reason she was expecting to see

Jeff standing there clutching a giant stuffed teddy bear. Or perhaps a bouquet of long stem roses. Instead, the door to her room opened painfully slowly to reveal...

A small boy sat in a wheelchair by the door. His right arm was in a cast, and his left leg was held out in front of him. His father, Jeff, was resting his right arm on the boy's left shoulder. Both were smiling.

Susan gasped and jerked the covers from her as she quickly sprang out of bed. For a second which seemed to last an eternity, she stood very still, holding on to the bed rail for support.

"Mommy!"

Susan sucked in her breath.

Suddenly Jeff was wheeling Timmy toward Susan who, in turn, dashed toward him.

The three of them embraced and Jeff said, "He's got a couple of broken bones, Susan. But he's okay. He's staying upstairs in the children's ward. Just as a precaution."

All Susan heard was that he's okay!

Susan cried and Timmy cried and Jeff cried. Even Bronson, standing some distance away, wiped a tear away, then quickly looked around to make sure no one saw him. He glanced back at Jeff and Susan and quietly left the room, closing the door behind him.

About The Author

ELSIE (L. C.) HAYDEN has been publishing since 1975 in various magazines, periodicals, and newspapers. To date, she has sold over four hundred pieces.

She holds a Master's Degree in Creative Writing from the University of Texas at El Paso. Besides writing, Mrs. Hayden enjoys drawing, reading, travelling, and scuba diving.

Mrs. Hayden, an English high school teacher, lives with her husband and two sons in El Paso, Texas, where she is at work on her next mystery/suspense novel, *WHEN COLETTE DIED*.